IMMORTAL SINS

A FANTASY ACADEMY ROMANCE

DARK FALLS ACADEMY

BOOK THREE

ANYA J COSGROVE

"Fire that's kept closest burns most of all."
-William Shakespeare

THE SECRET LOVERS

Allie

"Should I hang it behind the desk? Or is it too much?" Daniel Osbourne asks. He presses the forty-inch painting against the wall to show me the effect. The canvas depicts a battle sword with its silver blade parallel to the ground. Red dragon scales and swirling fire weave around the majestic weapon and spark a sense of pride in my heart.

Perched on the leather chair in the corner of the room, I give him a thumbs up. "Looks great there. It contrasts nicely with the white wall."

Dark Falls is ours.

Celeste Draco's old office needs to be spruced up. The midday sun spills between the seams of the closed blinds, and dust sticks in the air.

Dan puts the painting down and walks over to me. "What are you doing? Spying on your sister? Who cares if she dates some werewolf?"

The little blue dot signalling Jules' location pulses on the screen of Daniel's tablet. We were all tagged when we arrived at the Academy, so Daniel being headmaster allows me this perk. "Jules is not dating Jeremy, but she's been to his place four times in the last week. It's suspicious."

"Your sister is an angry kitten in a litter of wolf cubs. Even if she were to find out the truth about us, who would believe her?" He kneels in front of me and steals the tablet from my hands. "Now, why don't we christen this room properly?"

My eyes flick over to meet his playful gray stare, and warmth slithers inside my previously constricted chest. "You said she wouldn't derail our plans when she arrived, but then Cole took an interest in her, and we had to rethink everything."

With both hands around my face, he places a sweet kiss at the base of my jaw. "Which worked in our favor in the end. If your sister defends Cole now, everyone will think she's just another dumb girl in love with a Fae."

"It wasn't just Cole." I watch his expression closely for a tell, a sign that I didn't imagine his own interest in Jules. "Trent Darkwood, Lydia Hawks, Flynn Verinos, Olson Lewis, Miss Eillis—"

His index finger slices through the air and lands smack in the middle of my chest. "Don't say her name."

Realizing my mistake, I press on the shoulders of my dragon and bat my eyelashes. "Jules is more resourceful than you think. If she figures out that *I* used angel dust on Cole and not the other way around, people will rally around her."

"We still have some dust to bring her to our side." He picks me up to straddle him.

I scowl, my thighs stiff on each side of him. "You agreed not to use it on her. You *promised*."

"It's a last-resort option." He unbuttons my blouse. "But your sister isn't as smart as you think."

"Maybe you're right."

"I'm always right." Grinning from ear to ear, he deposits me on his large, mahogany desk. "We accomplished it all, my love. I'm headmaster of Dark Falls, and we have the horn in our possession. No one can touch us now."

Gosh, I hope he's right. Pray to the Dark Gods he is.

A loud knock startles us both, and Dan jumps away from me.

"Oz? Are you alone? I need to speak with you," Mr. Brady, the divination teacher and heart-throb horse shifter, says through the door.

I fumble with the buttons of my blouse, but Dan points to the desk. "Hide under it. Quick. Jack can't know you're here."

The legroom nook is twice as big as me, so I slip inside without a hitch. Light streams through a wide crack in the wood. I press my eye to it in time to see Mr. Brady walk into the room.

My boyfriend clicks his tongue. "What is it, Jack?"

The horse shifter tucks his hands in the pockets of his faded blue jeans. "We need to discuss the Fae students' situation. I've received quite a few pressing interview requests from Immortal News Today. Rumors fly that the students have been taken hostage."

I grin at that. Serves the elves right to be stuck here. Their so-called monarchs are apparently too busy to bother with their fate. Flynn and Jess don't hold enough political weight to deserve a swift rescue, and Dan's rise to power at Dark Falls means that their manipulative reign has finally ended.

Mr. Brady inches closer to the desk. "Their request to return home for a few days between the quarters has been denied."

Dan's legs block my sightline. "How does that equate to being held hostage?"

"They want to know when they can go home, boss."

I bite my bottom lip not to snort. Boo-hoo, I bet Flynn misses his mortal whores horribly.

"I can't let them go for now," Dan says.

Brady pauses, and a stuffy silence floats about the room before he adds, "May I ask why? We're risking a dire inter-realm incident."

The dragon's voice softens. "Jack, the incident has happened. It's done. Fae royalty has proven that they won't uphold our laws. If we want to keep them out of the Academy's administration, we can't enter negotiations from a position of weakness."

Brady clears his throat. "So Flynn and Jessa *are* hostages."

"They still have the same classes and opportunities as the other students. It's not like we forced them to enroll in this realm. They just can't leave for a while."

My line of sight clears.

Brady rubs the arch of his brow. "And how am I supposed to present that fact to them?"

"You just tell them that a long-standing Academy rule prevents students from leaving the realm as long as a security threat exists."

Exactly. It's no big deal. I hug my knees and rest my head on the wood. No one else will be hurt, and Flynn and Jessa will return home in time. I squeeze my eyes shut. Behind closed lids, I can almost see Miss Eillis' white, lifeless unicorn form.

A sickening shudder quakes my chest, and I shake my head to purge the unwanted memories.

"We're keeping them prisoners until that prince faces justice? We both know that's never going to happen," Brady grunts.

"Tell them whatever the fuck you want. They are not leaving until the President signs off on it."

Icy chills scatter along my neck.

"So, Darkwood is in charge of Dark Falls now, too? That's good to know..." Brady trails off.

Dan snorts, the sound low and vicious. "You're starting to sound like Rob Winslow. Be careful, Jack. Times are changing. You don't want to end up on the wrong side of this fight."

Magic sparks beneath my fingertips, and I sink my nails in my arm. If I'm not careful, I'll blow the desk right into the ceiling. Daniel and Dad will never see eye to eye on politics, but he's my father, and I love him. After I graduate, when we tell Dad about our relationship, I hope the two can mend fences.

"And what's the right side?" Brady asks.

"This side. Right here." Dan wraps an arm around his colleague's shoulders. "Don't worry, mate. The Fae won't stay here indefinitely.

We'll just use all the cards in our possession to get the best deal possible."

The quiet, slimy defiance in Brady's voice melts. "I trust you, Oz. You know that. But I heard that the old witch wanted to cancel Divination and…"

Dan smiles. "Would I let that happen to you?"

I hear the answering grin in Brady's tone. "Guess not." The horse shifter spins on his heels and heads for the door.

"Jack, one last thing," Dan breathes. "I wouldn't talk about Piper Davenport like that, if you know what I mean… But I got you, my friend. You have nothing to worry about."

I press a hand to my mouth to stifle a giggle. Mom's presence at the Academy ruffles many male egos.

Brady leaves, and I crawl from my hiding spot. Dan sits at the edge of his desk and waves me over. "Don't tell your mom about that. She's touchy about her age." His gaze falls to my exposed bra, and the smile on his handsome face turns wicked and self-serving. "Now, where were we?"

2

A JAR OF HONEY

Jules

"Why did you drag us here, Winslow?" Brie Demers says with her arms crossed, her back to the door. The bitter pout stuck on the mermaid's face chips away my confidence.

The oxygen is sparse in Jeremy's cramped bedroom, and I tug on the hem of my blouse, unsure I should have called this meeting after all.

Flynn leans against the desk, his hands on both sides of him, grasping the ledge. A loose tie hangs from his neck, and his white sleeves are rolled above his elbows. The bunch of his biceps and the golden glow of his skin set me on edge. His body seems too tall, his stature too grand, and his Fae beauty too bright for the narrow, dull and dusty space.

The boredom on his cherub-like face irks my temper.

Sitting cross-legged on the twin bed, Lydia steals glances at the Fae like a leprechaun watches his golden cauldron. Jeremy remains glued to her side, and his fists betray a hint of fur.

Five unlikely, reluctant allies, brought together more by circumstances than loyalty. The heavy metal posters glued to the wall make the small room seem even more crowded.

Dread fills my chest. "I asked you all to come here today because we're the only ones in the realm who believe that Cole isn't a murderer."

Flynn raises a brow. "Team Cole? Really? How uninspired."

Brie flashes a hint of teeth. "She's a proud girlfriend."

"Cole's army works better," Flynn cracks.

Brie buttons up her black jacket. "Listen, I did my part when I smuggled Cole out of the realm."

"Better yet, Flynn's harem—and the weird, antisocial murderous werewolf."

Jeremy growls. "Don't test me, Fae."

Flynn skips closer to him. "Oh, watch out, the big bad wolf who lives in a shoebox has anger issues."

Hand braced on my forehead, I zone out the boy's obnoxious chatter and speak directly to Brie, "You don't know the whole story."

"I don't need to know anything. Cole is safe. I'm out." She reaches for the doorknob.

Flynn stretches his arms above his head. "Verinos and Company has a nice ring to it."

"I'll bite your head off," Jeremy answers.

"Shut up, all of you!" Lydia shouts. "This isn't a prank, a stupid dare, or an exam. Miss Eillis was *murdered*, and we might be next if we don't figure out how to expose the real killer."

This stops Brie cold and wipes the mocking grin off Flynn's face.

Lydia tugs on her red braid. "Five doses. That's all we have left from the antidote she brewed before she died."

"We should each take one to make sure we haven't been compromised," Brie says.

Jeremy's fists uncurl, and his yellow eyes fly to the ground. "We should try another one on Allie."

Lydia bites down on her thumb. "One dose each will not get us far."

"Winslow should keep them." Flynn's voice booms across the room, free of the earlier snark. "She's the first one to testify in the trial. If Osbourne wants to seal Cole's fate, he'll start there."

Brie wrinkles her nose. "Professor Oz? What does he have to do with it?"

"You said you weren't interested," Flynn says.

I grip the Fae's elbow. "How do *you* know?" I had no intention of telling Brie or Flynn about Oz's involvement, not today. I still can't wrap my brain around the fact that my sister, Allie, is sleeping with him, let alone that she helped him murder Beth and framed Cole for it. Their plan was so masterfully executed, *I* almost fell for it. Allie must be under some type of evil influence—magical or otherwise. She'd do anything to earn her mother's love, something that should have been given away freely but she always yearned for, so maybe Piper manipulated her somehow. Some pieces of the puzzle are still missing.

Flynn swats my hand away. "You're not the only one with ties to Faerie." His breezy, self-satisfied demeanor tugs at a loose thread inside me.

"You talked to Cole?" I ask. "When?"

Flynn brings a finger to his mouth. "It's a secret."

It's been two weeks since I saw Cole in that grove on the equinox, and I haven't managed to contact him since. We both agreed that he was better off in Faerie, but the distance stings all the same.

It's not like I can FaceTime him, and letters are too dangerous, so I can't wrap my head around how Flynn communicated with him.

The roots of Brie's hair spark with lime-green highlights. "Oz is behind this? How?"

We catch Brie up on the general hypothesis.

"Oz has angel dust at his disposal, and we only have five antidotes. We're screwed. We need more." Her shoulders sag, and it's the first sign that she thinks of this secret meeting as more than an unpleasant interlude with frenemies.

"I've gone over this in my head a thousand times, and I agree with Brie. Could Deveraux replicate this? Find out the ingredients? Like a reverse-engineered recipe?" I ask.

Brie nods. "If anyone at Dark Falls can do it, it's her. She's the most esteemed Spells and Sorcery teacher in the three realms."

Flynn boosts himself on the desk, sitting with his legs spread wide. "Assuming she's not in on it, or affected by angel dust herself."

"She's immune. Beth said so. And I think she's our best bet." A dash of confidence blazes through my gut. There's no love lost between us, but we can work together. Like Lydia said, this is more important than petty school rivalries. This is life or death. With one whiff of angel dust, any of us could become a helpless pawn in Oz's twisted game.

I flip through my notes, hoping that the doodles and scraps of information will suddenly click together. "A unicorn's horn is an extremely rare and potent ingredient in many spells. Oz needs it for something. I just can't figure out what. Whatever he plans to do with it, we have to stop him."

Lydia grabs her notebook from the blue comforter. "Some references say that it's a powerful arcane focus for healing spells."

Jeremy wraps an arm around her shoulders. "I read it could be carved into a weapon to pierce the most potent magical armors."

Flynn pushes himself off the desk. "So basically, it can do anything. The holy uni-fucking-grail."

"Legends say that a unicorn can be reborn if its horn is recovered," Brie whispers, her voice low and ethereal.

A feverish heat travels from my ears to my chest.

Flynn sneers like he just lost his last thread of respect for the mermaid. "Have you lost your gills? Nothing can make someone come back from the dead."

Brie crosses her arms. "I'm just repeating what my grandmother said."

I place myself between them. "What else did she say?"

The stiffness in Brie's spine eases. "She told us the elders used to bring the fallen unicorns back to life."

Bringing Beth back from the dead...it's too good to be true, and yet, my heart swells. "No one can know about this. We can't tell anyone else about Oz, the antidote, or what we're trying to do. As long as we don't know how far up this goes and who can be trusted, we have to keep it secret." My gaze darts to Flynn. "We need to vow not to speak of this."

With a perfectly rehearsed air of faux-drama, he brings a hand to his chest. "You want *my* magic to solidify this freak show?"

I hold his stare.

He cocks his head to the side, his eyes the color of the ocean under a cloudless sky. "I do this for you, and you have to kneel whenever I tell you to. For a year."

I cringe at the giddiness in his voice. "A week."

His grin widens. "One month."

Blood rushes to my ears. Kneeling at Flynn's feet whenever he pleases is not my idea of a good time. "Fine. By the Dark Gods, I swear it."

We shake on it, and magic spirals in my bones.

He rubs his palms together. "Let's try this thing."

"We have no time—"

"Kneel, witch." The dark, luscious inflections of his voice radiate inside my cells. I grit my teeth together on the way down, but I have to obey.

A kid at Christmas holding candy...and chocolate...*and* chocolate candy comes to mind as he says, "This is fun."

"Fuck you, Verinos." I start to unfold.

"*Kneel,*" he repeats, denying me. He motions for the others to gather around me. "Alright, pinkie-swear time, children." With a wink, he offers Lydia his hand.

The seer holds her arms close to her chest. "We don't have to hold hands."

"A group deal is a bit trickier. Humor me."

Eyes glued to the floor, she reluctantly extends one hand, and Jeremy grabs the other. A sour taste invades my mouth. I press my palms on my thighs, stuck on my knees in the middle of the huddle.

Brie peels herself off the wall to join the circle. "What about Winslow? Does she have to swear, too?"

The tip of Flynn's black army boot grazes my nylons. "She's *knee-deep* in it, so I think it's fair for her to be excluded from the vow. And she needs to talk to Deveraux."

3

MERCURIAL

Jules

*L*ast quarter, the Spells and Sorcery class was cramped and busy. Now, half the students are gone. The murder and subsequent investigation, along with the Magisterium's continued presence on campus, have pushed quite a few students to take the quarter off. Since we're allowed to study at our own pace, the unexpected deferrals have been tolerated by the new administration.

I sit with Lydia at the front of the class. Vicious whispers echo at my back. Ever since the official witness list for the trial was leaked to the press, my name appearing at the top, wild theories and crazy conjectures follow my every step.

"Have you washed your bloody hands today, Winslow? Only a couple of weeks before you have to fess up in front of a judge," Mel quips happily from the desk behind me. Despite the fact that her father won the Presidential election because of this snafu, she insists on painting me as the villain of the story.

I ignore her completely to spite her.

Sunrise creeps closer and closer, orange and pink hues visible through the large windows. At five o'clock sharp, Deveraux strolls to her desk, ever so intimidating.

A classy black dress hugs her curves, and her ebony skin seems darker still. The usual glow of power around her sparks off every few seconds like she's carrying around a small—and very mean—personal thundercloud.

Standing with her back to us, a heavy sigh heaves her chest before she spins around. "What happened here last quarter was not only a tragedy, it was a shame. I lost a lifelong friend, and I expect you all to respect her memory with your silence. If I hear so much as one stupid rumor about what happened that night, a whiff of gossip about the upcoming trial, you will be asked to leave. Am I making myself clear?"

Students exchange tense glances, but no one dares to speak.

Deveraux taps the ground with her sleek, black heel. "Am I making myself clear?"

"Yes, Miss Deveraux," we all say in unison.

"I will assign the teams this quarter." She observes the class and pairs us up with a decided finger. Lydia and Brie get partnered, which could be interesting.

Deveraux knocks on the empty desk where Cole usually sits, and her eyes close for a fleeting moment.

Does she believe the rumors, or did she like Cole enough to give him the benefit of the doubt? The Fae prince was somewhat of a teacher's pet.

After a heavy pause, she says, "Julia, you're with Flynn."

Flynn serves me a bright smile as I join him across the aisle. "Kneel, witch."

"I hate you."

In front of everyone—everyone left, that is—I fall to my knees at the Fae's feet.

The pixie twins, my Summer Hall dormmates, gape, their mouths open too wide to laugh or judge me—which is a first. Melanie fails to stifle a growl with the back of her hand.

Hands on her hips, Deveraux tilts her head to the sky. "I'm not even going to ask."

To my surprise, Flynn offers me a hand to get up, but I stare ahead and wait for the magic to wane.

When it does, I climb onto the stool next to him and dump my heavy cauldron on his fingers.

"Ow!" He yelps, but the unaffected grin sticks to his lips. He leans in. "Now, if you'd always been that reasonable, we would have been quick friends."

A fresh, fruity scent tickles my nose. Accustomed or not to Fae glamors, Flynn's proximity leaves me lightheaded. While shadows flock to Cole to create mesmerizing patterns on his skin, Flynn's catches all the light in the room. The sunrise plays with the sinews of his muscles, and I catch myself staring at his ass. If I burned the back of his trousers while he cast a spell, would he feel it?

I bite back a snort at the mental image of Flynn walking around all day with his ass hanging out and force my attention back to Deveraux's instructions.

After class ends, I hang back, waiting for everyone to clear out so I can talk to the professor. The stormy aura of power around her almost drains the courage out of me, but I shove down the urge to flee.

She raises a hand in front of her when I approach the desk, not looking up from her grimoire. "Take it as a compliment. I trust you can handle a Fae, unlike many of your peers."

I unclasp my bag. "I came to talk about angel dust."

Her purple eyes snap up to meet mine.

"Miss Eillis managed to brew an antidote." Fingers cramped around the small bottle, I drag it out of the bag.

"She trusted you with this." It's not a question, but a fact. The glitch of thunder in her stance eases as she walks around the corner of her desk. "Beth mentioned that she was mentoring you, but I had no idea…"

I hand her the precious liquid. "Right before she died, she told me not to tell anyone about it, but I thought you should know." Trust doesn't come to me in spades, especially not these days, but my gut tells me Deveraux is worthy of it. "Is there a way to know how she made it? Can we replicate it?"

She raises the spell to the light and squints. "Maybe."

Bottom lip tucked between my teeth, I hesitate. "Beth said you were immune to angel dust."

Deveraux frowns, and I feel as though I'm posing—or being measured—for a dress. She slides a small key out of the bun at the nape of her neck and uses it to unlock a big chest at the front of the class. "I worked on a possible cure to angel dust day and night, and I couldn't get close to an antidote, but I did manage to cook something of importance."

Star-shaped red cookies with sprinkles sit prettily in a transparent Tupperware container. "This is a barrier spell. It won't dispel the effects of the angel dust already in your system, if any, but it will protect you from further harm. However, it will also block out any other spell from affecting you, so no basic dry spell, no stamina potion—anything that affects your body—will work while the barrier remains active. Its effects last about a day."

Eyes wide, I grasp the mundane container.

"Beth trusted you with her most treasured success, so you should take a batch," she adds with warmth.

"Thank you." If Deveraux somehow fell under Oz's power…magically or not… I shiver at the thought. The dessert looks innocuous enough. Usually, spells lose their powers and properties when they aren't properly bottled. "How did you manage to make them look so…normal?"

"I'm not the Spells and Sorcery teacher for nothing." She gives me a tentative, rare smile. "One more thing before you go. Headmaster Osbourne asked me about this." She reaches underneath her desk and retrieves a squared clay pot and…

My breath catches as I recognize my Fae seedling. The sight of the dry, saggy brown flower quickens my pulse. Withered. Dead. Useless.

After they confiscated it from my room, I tried, and failed, to track it down. If the flower was still intact, I could use it to track the horn.

The bottom part of the plant looks about to sigh its last breath, and I swallow hard.

"Oz couldn't figure out what it was, but I did. You're a talented witch, Julia, but fire burns, too. Casting an upside-down spell in this realm is dangerous."

The admonishment isn't as abrasive as I expected it to be.

"I wanted to catch the angel fruit thief," I admit with a defeated sigh.

Deveraux hands me the clay pot. "You could still try once it's healthy enough to bloom again. Feed it your blood twice a day, and ask Mrs. Pembrooke about Beth's personal collection. Tell her you have my permission. With the right cues, you won't end up in the infirmary."

"Thank you." I hold the seedling close to my chest. Deveraux is the only person who seems to grasp exactly how much trouble we are in. How much Beth's death *sucks*. "Can I ask you one more question?"

She tilts her head to the side. "Yes?"

"Why would someone risk everything to possess a unicorn horn?"

Deveraux presses a trembling hand over her breast. "Why are you asking *me*?"

"You know everything."

The intense, eerie vibe recedes. "Not everything." Deveraux spins around and discreetly wipes the corner of her eye. "I didn't know enough to save her."

A tight squeeze crushes my heart. On that front, Deveraux and I are kindred spirits.

Humidity rolls off the stone walls of the restricted section. The day is unseasonably hot, and the stacks of books reek of mildew and loneliness. Mrs. Pembrooke probably spent the whole day casting dry spells to spare the precious, brittle pages of the most coveted and important tomes in the realm.

The wings at the librarian's back twitch as she approves the list of books I requested, most of them part of Beth's collection. "Don't be fooled, I know what you're doing."

My shoulders tense. "Sorry?"

"There is no uglier crime than killing a unicorn." She inches closer and lowers her voice. "Were you really there when it happened?"

I've been asked about that night more times than I've got hairs on my head, but coming from Pembrooke...

"I can't believe he did it." The leopard-print glasses slide down the tip of her pointy nose. "He was always such a gentleman." With that, she flies up the staircase.

I head to my usual table. A black uniform jacket is sprawled over it, and I search the stacks for the intruder. Everyone knows this is my spot.

Trent appears, holding a pile of books to his broad chest. "Hey."

A tinge of fear pinches my belly, but his garnet eyes do not betray a hint of thirst. "Hey."

The books land on the table with a soft thud.

"Can we talk?" he asks.

With a quick nod, I sit on the stool across from him. The shorter haircut somewhat strips him of his carefree, rebellious vibe, and his anti-dress code leather jacket is nowhere to be found. The roundness of his cheeks isn't as pronounced as it used to be.

He drums an absent-minded pattern on his knee. "How are you? Really?"

"Wretched."

He scans the empty stacks. "Are you nervous about the trial?"

In another life, Trent and I might have shared secrets with each other, but I keep a neutral expression on my face.

He smacks his lips and traces a line in the wood with his nail. "I can protect you, you know."

I roll my shoulders back. *Protect* me? Last time Trent *protected* me, he tried to have me expelled for a crime I didn't commit. "You told me yourself you couldn't be seen with me."

"My father is a dick. I didn't have much of a choice, but it's over now." He puffs his chest. "If we hung out more, I'm sure the other students would back off. The stupid Fae is gone, Jules. It's in your best interest to distance yourself from that disaster." No matter how altruistic he tries to make it sound, the hard edge of his voice drips with contempt.

"I'm sure being your girlfriend would help my *reputation*." Ever since their father was elected, Mel and Trent's popularity and overall sway over the other students had skyrocketed.

He drags a tired hand over his face. "You think this is what I wanted? The press is constantly breathing over our shoulders. Melanie's affair with Flynn made the front page of Witch Tales last week. And that horrible primordialist woman basically lives in my house."

The last part grabs my attention. *Horrible woman* describes Allie's mother to a T, and while they now belong to the same political party, I didn't think Piper was close to the new President. "Piper?"

"Yeah, she's the worst. And it's obvious to anyone with eyes that he's banging her."

"Your dad…and Piper Davenport?" I repeat.

Trent purses his lips in disgust. "Ick, I know."

The cringey instinct to dismiss the internal images that flash in my brain at the mention of the two of them together gives way to a ticklish buzz. Theodore Darkwood and Piper Davenport… She's such a hypocrite. The last few years, she often denounced on national TV the damages that vampire feeding does to our fragile cohabitation with humans.

I guess that was before Darkwood embraced her rotten party to steal the election. Piper's ambition knows no bounds. If she somehow got into the President's ear—and pants—what a scary thought…

Trent scoots closer, and the stool's legs scratch along the carpet. "How is your dad handling his demotion?"

I keep my poker face on. "He got elected."

"Yes, but he's basically the only elementalist in office. That can't be fun."

I sidestep the issue entirely. Our past relationship does allow me some insight into his family, and I need to dig into that Darkwood-Davenport connection. "You told me before you didn't care much about politics. Your father has never been interested in high office before. What does he want?"

"Power. This election was carefully planned. He found a loophole in the previously airtight law that prevented him from running and blackmailed enough puppets to back him up."

I lean close to his ear and lower my voice. "How far is he willing to go to keep it?"

Trent chuckles bitterly. "If he had to sacrifice his own children, he wouldn't hesitate."

A shiver passes through me. Trent is not kidding, and while Oz is my number one enemy, Theodore Darkwood might be the head of the snake.

Our lips are a hair apart, and I can read in the pinch of his pout and the intensity of his stare how badly he wants to kiss me. I open my mouth to speak, but he just pulls away with a defeated sigh.

Before we became enemies, I used to love his fresh, cool kisses. I wish I could explain what really happened to Beth and recruit Trent to our side, but the vampire would never believe me. I'm afraid his prejudice against Faerie—against Cole—is too ingrained in his identity for him to switch sides.

4

DEMONS

Jules

Powdery leaves sprout in the Summer Hall gardens, but no amount of green could hide the hideous crime that took place here. The poison apple trees that were once so plentiful show dead twigs and a few blackened roots.

Next to the corded-off Magisterium section, branches and vines weave and crest in a beautiful arch. Rows and rows of thick, luscious white roses sag under the moonlight. The decadent bloom highlights the exact place where Beth died, and silvery rays dance across the silky petals.

Magus and High Council representatives came and tried to relocate the body, but mother nature buried the unicorn on her terms and built her an immovable shrine.

I hug my knees on the grass, my clothes protected from the evening dew by a dry spell. Uneven thumps wreck my heart. If only I'd tried harder to get through to Allie... If only I hadn't been so distracted…

Regrets coagulate in a hard mass inside my belly, and I fight off hot, useless tears. Zipping up my black hoodie, I sprawl out to a more comfortable position and study my notes until a familiar tingle raises all my hair up to attention.

My nostrils flare, and I stare into the night to spot the intruder. A dark mass moves through the electric-blue cedar edge, graceful and feral. The quality of the movement, the decisiveness in each step, does not belong to this world.

Onyx prances closer.

Shadows and light twinkle over black fur as the panther slumps over my outstretched legs.

I blink a few times, wondering if she's real. I haven't seen her since that fateful night Cole disappeared into the sea, almost believed she went with him.

The demon cat rests her head on the ground between her two front paws and closes her eyes. A soft, crackly mewl leaves no room for interpretation.

I raise a tentative hand to pet her head. "I get it. I miss him, too." If she was human, I couldn't have admitted it, but I trust her more than the beasts that rule this damn school.

Onyx's whiskers bristle before she sniffs my punctured finger. The Fae seedling fed voraciously yesterday. I bet the wound smells of Faerie, like her master. She rubs the crest of her skull against my hand and purrs. The geometrical, shimmering fur feels fresh and crunchy.

Two demons under the stars, pining for a Fae prince. I can't help but think it would make for a hauntingly depressing mermaid song. A pink tongue darts out of Onyx's mouth, and she licks her big paws, claws retracted. I reach for my notes.

Beth's personal collection contained a treasure chest of information on Fae plants, some of the chapters written by the unicorn herself. I couldn't leave the library with most of them, but I transcribed the sections on the upside-down tree. According to Beth's notes, a few ingredients from Cole's grimoire are too volatile for this realm and should be substituted for others. The spell will guide me to an object of my choosing with the help of an arcane focus. Beth's input, even from beyond the grave, is invaluable. Once the seedling is strong enough to bloom again, I'll find her horn and figure out what Oz plans to do with it.

If somehow, it could be used to save her...

My pulse quickens. I've read all I could find in the library about unicorns, but Brie's legend that one could be brought back to life remains unsubstantiated. I did learn more about their kind, their culture. The only known horde in existence relocated to an undisclosed location after being chased out of their lands. It's been so long since the last sighting that most people believe they are extinct. Of course, these people didn't know Beth was one.

I think back to what she told me about the Dryad war, about Dark Falls' unexplainable power source, and how she'd been asked to stay and keep watch on the grounds after her kind left. If only I'd discovered her true nature when she was still alive, maybe I could have understood the lesson she meant to teach me quicker.

I don't sleep much these days, haunted by what might have been.

Onyx's presence re-energizes me, my mind crisp, and my stiff muscles painless.

I dust off my pants and follow Onyx past the line of trees, using them as cover to practice. Beth's training shouldn't go to waste.

The sphere of infernal magic I used to fry the death spell meant for Cole was a surprise, but the memory of its power still crackles in my fingertips. Sweat pearls on my forehead as I try to summon a fresh one, using Beth's breathing exercises and soothing voice as focus.

The volatile, elusive magic arches between my fingers, but I struggle to shape it into a worthy projectile.

Onyx's tail twitches whenever I get close. After a while, she sinks her claws deep into a small, nearby tree.

I pause. "What's wrong with the tree?"

Air blows out of her muzzle, and she gives me a decisive slice of the head, effectively motioning for me to try and cut the tree down.

My brows pull together, and I concentrate on the claw marks and the rough bark instead of trying to mold the magic into an orb. A slash of purple energy axes the tree in two, and the top part cracks and tumbles to the ground.

The jaguar mewls.

A wide grin stretches my lips. I eye the demon cat up and down. "Thank you for the tip, Onyx."

The moon reaches for its peak in the night sky when I finally head for bed.

The sliding door squeaks behind me.

A human shape is hunched over the table. My fire scurries to the surface, and the glow warms Allie's drowsy face.

I yelp. "What the fuck? It's the middle of the night!"

Rubbing her eyes, she jumps to her feet. "You stayed outside a heck of a lot longer than I expected. I fell asleep." She discards her tea mug in the sink, her notes sprawled on the table behind her like she's been waiting for me to come in for *hours*.

She's not allowed to be here, so far away from her dorm, at this hour, but I guess breaking the rules is fair game when you're fucking the headmaster.

I tap my foot on the ground. "We shouldn't talk in here. Let's go back outside."

"No!" Her gaze flies to the ground. "Not outside. In your room, maybe?"

All this time, she waited in here… Why not come out and talk to me out in the gardens? Unless the sight of Beth's tomb makes her squirm.

"Jules…" She tucks her blond hair behind her ears. "The trial is coming up. I'm nervous as hell. I wanted to see how you were."

"Peachy." I shouldn't show how much her betrayal affects me. I should play it cool, lay into the victim masquerade, but I can't. Not when we're alone in Summer Hall's kitchen, surrounded by Beth's things.

Her blue eyes dim. "Don't be cruel. Cole killed her, not me."

My teeth grit together. "I know."

She searches my gaze as though she's both looking for forgiveness and testing my resolve. "Then why are you so angry?"

From the first day I stepped foot at Dark Falls, Allie has lied to me, and I saw right through her feigned aloofness. She sees right through me now.

There it is. Sister vs sister. Winslow vs Winslow.

Blue blood princess vs demon child.

"You lied." No amount of tacked-on honey could sweeten my dry, hollow tone. "You let him use you."

Allie's chest heaves. "Cole?"

A heavy, delayed breath blows through my lips. "Your boyfriend."

Something passes between us. Allie and I used to excel at silent quibbles, arguing so quietly behind Dad's back that he didn't intervene.

Her nostrils flare. I bite my tongue.

She crosses her arms around her tight frame. "I didn't have a choice. Fae don't belong here. Not long ago, you would have agreed. They made life miserable for us mortals. They attacked us *first*."

"Beth wasn't a Fae." I press my tongue behind my teeth not to say more.

At that, a previously hidden layer of guilt and anguish shines just enough on Allie's grief-stricken face for us to understand each other. It's clear as day she feels remorse for what she did.

How could she shun everything she loved in favor of a devious man? I wish I could lay it all out in the open, but she'd just run, like always. Before I push her buttons any more, I need to gather enough information to drill some sense back into her. Allie won't rot in prison for someone else. If she believes she's in real danger, there might be hope to crack her open, yet.

5

A HORSE'S KINK

Jules

"Step back, mortal," Flynn says with a self-aggrandizing sigh. He caresses the door leading to Oz's old office with great—and weirdly intimate—care. A smooth magic ring slowly stretches to life near the doorknob. The Fae passes a hand through the solid pane as though it's no big deal and twists the lock open.

The door squeaks on its hinges. I screen the doorway for an active spell, but find only dust and gloom.

Flynn grips the crown molding above the door and lifts himself off the ground, swinging into the room like raw nerves on legs. "Now, if you were a unicorn horn, where would you be? Not here; I say."

The restless, show-off energy unnerves me. "You bug me."

He dashes forward, his feline movements slick and quiet. "You asked me to come."

"I didn't." I lock the door behind us. Most of the books, folders, and pictures are already gone, but a few cardboard boxes lie on the desk, and I walk over to them.

"You asked with your eyes," Flynn says.

I shoot him a death glare wrapped in poisonous honey. "Tell me. Am I asking anything with my eyes right now?"

His school-girl giggle sparks flames under my palms.

I'll take a restless, jumpy Flynn over the malicious and cruel one, but I can't understand why he came. "If anything, you being here jeopardizes my chances. They're watching you."

"The Magus he tasked with surveillance are dumb. They don't seem to realize I can basically walk through walls."

Flynn's ability to carve portals into the ether allows him to travel through solid matter, or basically teleport behind someone—a skill he loved to use to thoroughly kick my ass in the Duel ring. One second he's in front of you, and the next, he steps through a fresh portal behind you and trips you up.

I open an unlabeled box. Oz's whole life is relevant to this search. Even if the horn isn't here, any information on him could become vital. "How do you summon those portals?"

Flynn cracks his knuckles. "Dimensional rings."

I roll my eyes. "How do you summon those *dimensional rings?*"

"How do you summon fire?"

"It's not something you learned in Faerie?"

"Nope." He emphasizes the word with a loud, obnoxious pop and sifts quietly through the drawers without disturbing anything.

My brows raise. "You make a good spy."

"Lots of practice."

I eye him sideways, wondering if he's kidding, but before I can ask, a loud knock resonates behind us. My gaze flies to the closed door.

"Daniel?" The voice is male, but I can't quite place it.

Flynn whispers a quiet, "Fuck."

I hold my breath.

"I know someone's in there. Open the door, or I will." Mr. Brady's threat rains across my shoulders like an ice storm.

Flynn abandons the folders and joins me by the main desk. In one

26

swift movement, he works his button-down shirt open. The familiar tattoos on the golden planes of his chest delay my response by a millisecond. They're identical to Cole's.

I hiss under my breath.

He jerks his chin at the door.

I swallow hard, understanding his plan. He boosts me on the desk, and I wrap my thighs around him. My breath catches when he buries his fingers in my hair like it's the most natural thing to do.

The doorknob rattles.

I know what comes next. It's the second time that a kiss between us doesn't count. I still want to whip him for the first. He leans in until we share breath but stops, as though asking for my permission.

I give him a small nod, and he presses his lips to mine. Compared to the kisses we shared while I was under the thrall of the love potion, this one doesn't sicken me—or compel my magic to burn him.

Flynn's tongue darts out to tease my bottom lip. Arms linked behind his neck, I kiss him back. There are so many reasons why I shouldn't be doing this, shouldn't allow it, shouldn't *enjoy* it, but none of them comes to me in that moment, the guilt squashed by the subterfuge.

"Flynn. What the fuck?" Brady asks.

My eyes snap open, and I hide behind a veil of curls.

"The office was empty," Flynn drawls, not giving me an inch of space, my legs still wrapped tightly around his midriff.

Brady's aggressive stance melts. "You need to be careful. If someone caught you here…"

The Fae shrugs. "Oz was always such a prick about his office being private. I couldn't resist."

"He's headmaster now." He doesn't look twice at me or address me in any way, a fact that simply enrages me. To him, I'm just another girl that fell under Flynn's charms.

"Makes fucking on his desk even better." Flynn rubs a fiery path up my thighs and below the hem of my skirt. His fingertips graze the edge of my nylons.

I grab his wrists and peel him off me. "Enough. Let's go to your room."

With a barely contained chuckle, Flynn laces our fingers. "Yes, ma'am."

Three steps outside the office, he pins me to the wall and kisses me stupid. I clench my fists, but Brady must still be in eyesight, so I continue to play along.

The Fae kisses the slope of my neck thoroughly. Selfishly. Eyes fixed on his dark tattoos, I run a trembling hand across his bare chest.

The answering growl softens my legs.

A husky pant caresses my ear. "You know you can't just summon him here by touching his mark, don't you?" He squeezes my hips and grinds against me in a scandalous fashion before releasing me and luring me deeper into Winter Hall's labyrinth.

My stomach churns with fire and nerves. Once we are definitely out of sight, I press a hand to my mouth. "Why so much?"

"Brady caught me with many girls before, and he likes to watch. I figured leaving him horny as hell would make him more amenable. He won't tell anyone what he saw now."

I struggle to find my breath. "Do you hear yourself?"

"Do you feel your pulse right now, witch?" He raises my wrist in front of my eyes, his thumb flat on my artery. "You turned into a puddle the second you saw my tattoos."

"You didn't have them at the beach games." I've seen Flynn half naked before, and I'm positive he didn't have the tattoos.

"I *masked* them at the Beach Games." He swings open the door to his room. The motion reveals a cozy, somewhat large dorm with a queen-sized bed in the middle and a desk with two chairs in the back.

Jessa, Cole and Flynn's female counterpart, lounges with her head propped over Flynn's pillows. She snaps her book shut as we come in. An intricate blue braid wraps around her head in a beautiful, old-fashioned design, and her fair skin contrasts with the red duvet like the crisp white flesh of an apple.

The taste of Flynn's kiss—strawberries, champagne, and shame—lingers on my tongue.

Her stunned gaze settles on my disheveled hair before it bounces over to Flynn. "Not you, too. Is the entire male population blind or something?"

"Hey, Jess." Flynn releases me, unfazed, and grabs a water bottle from the small refrigerator tucked underneath his desk.

Jessa jumps off the bed and stalks closer. "The rumors about you are true. A Fae whore, nothing more."

The insult shreds through my dignity and pride. That's exactly what I feared would happen, but I'd rather endure vile gossip for the rest of my life than be a puppet in Oz's game. If that's the price I have to pay, I'm good with it.

I brace my hands on my hips. "What about it, Tinkerbell?"

Jessa's perfectly-shaped blue eyebrows bend in a cruel, condescending manner. "You must give really good head."

A hollow smile colors Flynn's face. "You want to watch?" He sits at the edge of the bed, his elbows resting on his thighs. The predatory look on his face scatters tremors down my spine.

I'm frozen in place, torn between the need to head for the door and the devious, tantalizing urge to feed Jessa's obvious jealousy. I reach for the water bottle in Flynn's hands and swallow a few mouthfuls.

"Ugh. No, thank you," Jessa squeaks.

Flynn picks a piece of lint off my skirt. "Too bad. You could learn something."

I press the back of my hand to my mouth not to spit water out. Jessa's horrified grimace warms my ears and neck.

"Why are you here, Jess?" he asks.

"We're hostages, Flynn. *Pri-son-ers.*" She enunciates slowly as though he's too dumb to understand.

He waves her worries away with a nonchalant hand. "We're fine. They'll find a way to bring us home soon enough."

"You're useless." Jessa slams the door shut behind her.

Flynn runs the back of his index finger down my thigh. "You must stay at least two hours if everyone is to believe we had sex, so maybe we might as well—"

29

"Gods!" I step away from him.

Like he flipped off a switch, the playful, devil-may-care attitude vanishes, and he serves me a distant nod. "This is good for our cover."

He bounces off the bed and sits at his desk. The chair squeaks under his weight, and I peek at his papers. A familiar calligraphy immediately catches my attention, and my heart flip-flops. "What is this?"

He quickly covers the letter with his hand. "None of your business."

I form a dangerous hypothesis. "Cole wrote you a letter about Oz? Are you insane? The Magisterium reads every note that comes in or out of Dark Falls and tests it for enchantments."

"This is no letter. It's an ancient Fae stela." Flynn guards the text like a ghoul guards her younglings. "During a Faerie blood moon, the inscriptions leave one stela and appear on its twin."

"You and Cole are penpals?" Sweat gathers on my palms. Flynn had access to Cole all this time, and Cole never mentioned it, or even implied we could communicate this way? Why?

Flynn shuffles a stack of papers over the stela. "Cole and I are a lot of things."

I swallow hard. Cole somewhat denied he was having sex with Flynn.

There would be nothing wrong or particularly surprising about it, given the boys' reputations, but for reasons I can't explain, the idea fascinates me. It tugs at something deep in my belly and sparks fire on my neck like nothing else.

I sit on the empty chair next to Flynn and gauge his reaction. "Have you slept with him?"

His knuckles twitch over the desk. "Have you?"

Heat gathers on my cheeks. "Yes." It's a cold, hard fact, and denying it will only make me look foolish. But he doesn't need to know I'm in love with Cole.

Flynn twists in his chair to face me. "Wow. You admitted it. I didn't think you would."

His radiant smile trips my brain up.

I lick my lips. "And you?"

He leans in until our foreheads graze, his intense blue gaze fixed on mine. "He's my prince."

My pulse flutters. I want to know more, but I settle for the dark, hungry expression on Flynn's face.

6

THE COLD EMPEROR

Allie

The guest suite in Council Hall is the most secure, exclusive place in the realm. A crystal chandelier twinkles above my head. The menu for the upcoming seven-course dinner lies flat on the chic, round table in the dining room. Silver and gold watermarks shine over its surface, and I quietly fold it into a swan.

A gush of air whooshes from my palm as I raise the swan into the air and levitate it inside the chandelier until its wings are safely tucked between two crystals. My lips quirk.

Heels click along the lacquered hardwood. "Don't slouch, dear."

My spine straightens, and I smooth the skirt of my dress again.

Mom sits on the empty chair next to mine and crosses her ankles. She pours us both a cup of tea, and her manicured nails skim the porcelain. "Has Daniel adjusted to his new role?"

Fragrant jasmine vapours swirl into the air.

"He's amazing." I blow on the hot tea. "Did the potion help?" From the corner of my eyes, I check the tint of her skin, pleased to see no dark circles under her eyes—or a ridiculous amount of make-up meant to cover them.

"Yes. I feel much better."

A knot pulses in my stomach. "How long will it last?"

She pats the back of my hand. "Don't worry. As long as we have the horn, the sickness will not progress."

I reach for a fluffy pistachio macaroon, but Mom quietly taps the table, and I let my arm fall to my side. She's right. I shouldn't eat. Vampires use food as distractions for humans. I must show that I'm above such tricks, above my basic human needs.

When President Darkwood waltzes through the door, Mom rises to her feet, and I do the same.

The tall vampire's salt-and-pepper beard pulls attention away from his dry, hollowed-out cheekbones. Age doesn't show on an immortal's face very often, but Darkwood has been under a massive amount of stress and scrutiny.

I offer him a polite, demure smile.

"Nice to finally meet you, Allison."

"Mr. President." I offer a quick curtsy.

He gives Mom a quick peck on the cheek and motions for us to sit. His assistant, a lanky vampire with round glasses, lurks over the threshold of the dining room.

The butler comes to greet us and offers a wide selection of Pixie wines, but I only wet my lips in the red, velvety liquid. Pleasantries are exchanged, and I peek at the swan in the chandelier while mom and her lover chat about the latest council gossip.

When the conversation shifts to the trial, the blood drains from my face.

Theodore Darkwood laces his long fingers over the table. "Allison. Your mom and I want to make sure that you feel supported. I know the trial will bring back ugly memories, so if you need anything, anything at all, don't hesitate to ask."

"I'm okay. I'm ready." The appetizers arrive, but my mouth dries up at the sight of the rare beef medallion.

The vampire's fork sinks into the dark, juicy piece of meat, and blood leaks onto the plate. "How do you think your sister's testimony will go?"

Mom gives me an encouraging smile. She wants me to say that everything will be fine, but my conversation with Jules did nothing to ease my fears. She knows something, and I'll be damned if I don't grab this unprecedented opportunity to speak my mind.

"I don't know," I say, wiping the honeyed smile off Mom's lips.

She inches closer to me. "Allison, dear."

I tilt my chin up. "I told Daniel many times, and I'm telling you again. No matter how much you want me to say that Jules is in the dark, that she bought my story completely and will claim far and wide that Cole is a murderer, I'm not convinced."

Mom skims Darkwood's arm with her hand. "Theo, the little witch wouldn't dare speak against you."

The blood-red gaze brings a chill to my core, but the president ignores mom, his attention solely focused on me. "Go on."

I square my shoulders. "Jules is like a dog with a bone. She got too close to Cole, and she won't rest until she gets answers, no matter the cost."

"What answers could she get? Cole killed the unicorn, no?" His voice is dangerous.

"Yes, sir."

Darkwood waves his assistant over and whispers a few words in his ear.

Mom scratches her nails along the intricate lace of the tablecloth, but I stare defiantly ahead. I've tried to warn her many times, and she dismissed my insight as though Jules could never thwart her plans or defy her.

I know my sister. I tried to warn her about Cole, but she loves nothing more than chasing her own doom. If Mom couldn't keep her out of Dark Falls, nothing will stop her.

7

BAIT

Jules

The turrets of Summer Hall's tower allow for the sunset to slip through the cracks of my closely-knit blinds. The slivers of orange light hurt my eyes after another gloomy day in the library.

Lydia paints her nails a vibrant shade of red on my bed, a gelled toe spacer between her toes. "Whatever you're doing with Flynn is working. Vivianne told everyone you two were screwing like bunnies, and no one suspects a thing."

Sitting astride my desk chair in the narrow space between the bed and the clutter of homework, I fail to repress a grunt. "Yay?"

Her green eyes flick to me for a moment before returning to her pedicure. "Unless you two are going at it like bunnies..."

I slap her thigh.

"Hey, careful!" She shoos me away with her free hand. A swipe of nail polish smears her big toe. "I still can't look at Flynn. He makes me want to puke and undress at the same time—it's confusing."

I rest my chin on the back of the chair. "Puking while undressing sounds complicated indeed."

The seer screws the polish shut and sets it aside. "There's a whiff of fire on your ears, girl. Did something happen?"

My gaze flies to the ground, and my dark curls create a veil between us. "Brady caught us together in Oz's old office. We had to... improvise." The trial is a few days away, and I've got no clue what I'm supposed to say. I don't need the Flynn situation to spice that soup of emotions. I don't know exactly when the shift took place, but Flynn no longer sets my teeth on edge with disgust. Things simply changed between us.

Lydia cringes. "Be careful. Mel is going to want your head on a spike."

"She can get in line." Cole and his best friend plague my thoughts. White-hot images sprout in my overactive brain. Mel planted the seeds first, and the Fae stela and Flynn's cryptic answer only watered the weeds.

My palms get sweaty just thinking about the kiss. It's not the same as with Cole, but it's not harmless either. Am I into Flynn because he's Fae? What does it say about my attraction to Cole that I enjoyed kissing his best friend?

Is it merely lust that draws me to Cole?

No. The deal between us is done, but his voice still plagues my thoughts, and I dream of him every single night. Whatever I feel for him is real. Annoying, maybe. Impractical, absolutely—mopping around school because the Fae prince you're hot for is falsely accused of murder *sucks*.

The Fae plant near the foot of the bed stretches happily in the sun. A small bud has appeared at the end of a frail stem, and I get up to observe it more closely. Its leaves bristle as I come near. "The seedling will bloom soon."

After being nursed back to health by a pint of blood, the Fae plant might finally pay off.

Lydia trades her nail polish for a quill and slides her notebook out of her bag. "Do we have everything for the upside-down spell? I wish the administration would approve my request to move back in here. It would be so much easier to see each other."

I offer my finger to the seedling, and it latches on hungrily. "Would your parents approve?"

The quill pauses on the page, and Lydia shrugs. "I'm an adult. I told them their incessant meddling got in the way of school, so they backed off. A bit."

"Good for you. What about Jeremy? I saw you two holding hands…"

She shakes her head forcefully. "Jeremy is a friend. I'm done playing second fiddle to your sister, and I need a better boyfriend—preferably one who hasn't almost killed his ex-girlfriend in a fit of rage."

"Boo. That rules out pretty much every guy at Dark Falls."

She snorts into her hand.

A soft knock on the door stops the conversation cold.

No one ever visits me here besides Lydia, and my dormmates are hateful.

"Julia? It's me," Oz says through the door.

Lydia grips her inked feather so hard, I think it'll splint.

I crack open the door. "Hello, professor," I say with as much pep as I can muster.

The newly appointed headmaster offers me a meek smile. "How are you?"

"Good—Sure—Great—I'm okay."

Real smooth, Winslow.

"I didn't know you had company." He lowers his voice and leans in. "You should come to my cabin Friday night. I know how nerve-wracking a public trial can be. I'll help you prepare your testimony."

Now that I know what he did and how he operates, I see beyond the cool, relaxed, professor mask.

Each calculated word rolls off his tongue in a crafted illusion of warmth and accessibility. Oz makes you feel heard and important.

He's not a teacher that asks trick questions and reminds you of your incompetence. Every bit of his persona, down to the understated clothes, and the approachable body language, puts you at ease.

Only his gray stare betrays the intensity, the hunger. The deviance.

I wonder how he seduced my sister. Did he start with long looks and innocent brushes with her, too? He literally enchanted a blanket to make students feel safe, so nothing should surprise me.

"Yes, thank you, professor." The urge to clench my jaw becomes so potent that I fake a yawn to get rid of a cramp. "What time?"

He peers around the room behind me. "Eight thirty."

My pulse spikes. If he spots the seedling... I brace my arm on the doorframe and plaster a bright smile on my face. "I'll be there."

Loud steps echo up the stairwell as Oz leaves, and I'm not sure he bought my carefree act. My heart in knots, I close the door and hurry back to the bed.

"We might not get another chance to enter his cabin. Could we cast the upside-down spell before Friday? If the horn is in the cabin, we could steal it then," Lydia suggests. "If it's not in the cabin, we could still take advantage of his meeting with you to break into whatever vault he keeps it in."

"It's a tall order. Last time, it took three days for the bud to bloom."

The seer plays with her fingers. "Okay, but if we could locate it in time, how are you going to steal it?"

I avert my gaze. "Flynn assured me he could get inside any earth-made safe."

A wolfish smile spreads on Lydia's glossy lips. "Your ears are red again."

"Shut up." I throw a pillow at her face, but fire warms my ears.

Flynn's kisses shook me. Whenever I think of our make-out session, I picture his tattoos—and Cole's—and how crazy close they must have been when they had them done.

Cold shower for one, please.

AN OVERSIZED T-SHIRT hooks around my ankle, and I shake it off with a scoff. Jeremy's cluttered room has somehow become our rebel base. You'd think the wolf would have learned to pick his clothes up off the floor, but nooooooo.

Thursday night rolled around too quickly.

"Lydia and I checked the cabin this morning for active enchantments, and the place lit up like a fortress. The horn must be there. The seedling bloomed. I'm ready to cast the upside-down spell," I say to the group.

Jeremy and Lydia are sitting on the bed, as usual, while Brie swivels in the desk chair. Flynn sneers by the door like he's repulsed by the mess.

Lydia checks the spell's ingredients one by one on a piece of parchment. "We should split. Two of us will go with Jules while the others make sure Oz is still in his office."

Flynn steals the list from Lydia's hands. "I'm with the mortal. I want to know what else the dragon is hiding."

Brie tilts her hip to the side. "If I didn't know any better, I would believe the rumors."

"What rumors?" Flynn asks.

Tongue tucked below her right canine, Brie grins and takes a dramatic pause. "That you're encroaching on crown-land."

Flynn glances up from the parchment with a grin—feral and dry. "Must suck to reside in neutral territory."

Brie flips him off.

Lydia packs up the cauldron and spell gear. "It's settled. Brie and Jeremy can go to the office and keep an eye on Oz."

"I'll go." The mermaid answers, her pointed gaze fixed on the wolf. "Alone."

Jeremy growls in response.

Lydia, Flynn, and I hike from Night Hall to the trail that loops closest to Oz's cabin. Ferns sprinkle our path with the earthy scent of fresh dew while melted snow rustles down the streams and brooks from the mountain. My boots leave deep imprints in the mud. Spring at Dark Falls comes quicker than I'm used to, but it's also messier, like most things about this damn school.

Once we arrive within view of the cabin, Lydia holds Cole's Fae grimoire open to the right page, and I unpack the ingredients. Flynn sets up the cauldron.

I've prepared the spell and studied the steps. Compared to the work Cole and I did last quarter, it's going to be quick. Either the upside-down spell will allow me to see through the ether, or I'll go down like a rock.

After offering the Fae seedling one last meal, I pluck the one-petal flower off its body, and the whole plant curtsies in reverence.

"Creepy," Flynn says, inches from my face.

The proximity startles me. "Shh."

He holds his palms up in front of him and gives me an inch to spare.

With a decisive nod, I crush the petal inside the mortar and stir it into Lydia's cauldron. She adds in mistletoe and honey, along with a dash of lizard blood. The liquid turns bright red, and I scoop it up with a small silver ladle.

"Here goes." I raise the potion to my lips.

Darkness thickens around me, and in an instant, Lydia and Flynn melt into the background.

The thick brown bark of the trees stretches into a blotch of muddy colors. I'm walking both in and on a cloud—a dream within a dream —shapes and sounds slightly askew.

The woods, the sky, my own feet...the whole world is murky as hell. Light blooms in patches around the cabin like my eyes blended with a thermal camera. I paw at the space in front of me.

"Are you okay?" Lydia holds me steady, her slender, feminine hand holding mine tight.

The cabin flashes in and out of view in synch with the rapid beats of my heart. Fluorescents prints appear on the wet grass in front of me as though my eyes are seeing every single footstep—human and animal—that was ever taken in front of the cabin. It's too much information and colors for my brain to process. I blink rapidly and grab my forehead. "Whoa."

A large, hot hand settles at the small of my back as Flynn asks, "What do you see?"

I wet my lips. "Not much. *Too much.*"

He squeezes my free hand. "Your eyes are all white. It's really freaky."

If I cast this spell wrong and end up blind...my pulse quickens. "Give me Beth's mug."

The arcane focus will condense my attention over what I'm searching for. The mug Beth always drank her tea from should do the trick, and I placed a few petals from her grave into it to strengthen my connection to her memory.

Lydia guides my fingers around the ceramic handle, and the blurry kaleidoscope of colors finally stills. Small shoe prints rise out of the mass. They zigzag from the cabin's door and back to the trail a few times. Soft, light steps. Beth's steps.

Every single one of them.

A heavy breath wheezes out of my lungs, and I follow the trail to the cabin's door. The smoky shape of a hand—a skeletal reminiscence of her physical body—twists open the knob.

The cabin's entrance is guarded by a powerful alarm spell, but the ghost fragments of Beth don't trigger them. I'm tempted to follow but know better, so I head toward the large windows instead.

Beth's silhouette prances around the main room of Oz's cabin, her long white hair braided over her shoulder. The translucent apparition is blurry, but my heart pangs all the same. All the times she came here, every step she took, and all the laughs she shared in this small cabin are condensed into this eerie, macabre replay.

After a few heart-breaking, atrocious minutes, the ghost glides through the bedroom door. I tiptoe around the cabin to the bedroom window, Flynn's hand still steady in mine. Thick blinds obscure the inside of the bedroom.

My stomach lurches. "Fuck, I lost her."

Flynn brushes my shoulder. "Allow me." I can't see him, but his heat seeps through my skin despite the spell.

Lydia gasps. "It might trigger the alarm."

"Then we'll run," he says.

"I'm not sure—"

I clench my teeth. "Do it."

Flynn remains invisible to me, but the blinds are slowly pulled aside and allow a wide view of Oz's bed. Fresh, angry tears blur my vision, and sweat trickles down my neck. I do not want to think about Beth being in this bed, about Allie...

Next to the queen-sized mattress, Beth's ghost condenses into complete corporeal form, her body no longer translucent. A rictus of fear and pain deforms her peaceful features. In the middle of her forehead, a gigantic hole oozes blood. The red trickle is thick as syrup, ten times darker than it ought to be.

The boulder stuck in my throat presses my windpipe. This is no longer a remnant of her past, but a fragmented piece of her present. Her horn must be very close to the bed.

Beth slumps to the ground, and I observe the floorboards. An eerie light emanates from the spot right below her ass, and my eyes suddenly see through the hardwood, to a thick, metallic blue safe almost identical to the one Dad had at home for his High Council documents. A Magisterium safe.

Beth gives me one long, haunted look, before she curls over and hides her face in her knees, her green dress in pieces around her calves. Rocking back and forth, she shudders as the door behind her cracks open.

A long wisp of white smoke seeps through the doorway. The newly formed cloud hangs in the air for a moment before it takes shape, swimming through the room like an eel. The spectre whips toward the window, slithering closer, and hisses. Sharp teeth glisten in its mouth.

I'm almost certain it saw me, too.

I recoil from the apparition. I've seen something like it before. The first time I spotted Onyx in the woods, the demon had a similar depth and texture, but she was black instead of white.

Before I can move or speak, the mug is snatched from my hands.

A loud *clank* erupts through the trees, and my vision returns to normal.

Lydia shatters the arcane focus under her foot.

Fire swirls underneath my skin, and I fall flat on my ass in the wet grass. Water seeps inside my jeans, and goo smears my hands. "Why did you pull me back?"

Lydia tugs on her red ponytails. "Something appeared in the window. A nether being. It raised its claws toward you. It was trying to pull you in. Is the horn in there?"

Flynn waves his hand up and down in front of Lydia's face. "Are you high? A nether being?"

Hot tears glide down my cheeks. "It's there. Under the bed. Under the floorboards. She's trapped there."

"The horn?" Flynn offers me a hand to get up.

I grunt as he pulls me to my feet. A tremor of helplessness and disgust quakes my body. "No. Beth's soul."

8

OVER THE RAINBOW

Jules

"We have to steal the horn." My teeth chatter as I speak, the whiplash from the upside-down spell still thick in my veins.

Lydia wraps a second blanket around my shoulders, but I can't get the tremors to stop. I feel cold and lightheaded and numb. The tips of my fingers prickle as though I've been plunged into a tub of ice.

We regrouped in Jeremy's room to share the results of our investigation, and while Brie and Jeremy seem content that I localized the horn, they do not grasp the magnitude of our discovery.

"We can't leave it there." I turn to Brie. "Your grandmother wasn't so wrong about it. It's alive. Beth's soul is still attached to it, and she's in danger."

"Danger?" Jeremy asks.

"Something else was there. It didn't have a clear shape, but it was white and smoky and it felt our presence," Lydia explains. "It wasn't from this plane."

Brie purses her red lips. "Never mind the weird ghost shit—or the fact that neither beings don't actually exist—how are we going to break into Oz's cabin?"

"He invited me. If we could get him to leave me in there for a few minutes—"

She rakes her sharp nails against her nylons. "You think Oz is just going to leave you in his cabin alone?"

"If we create some sort of big emergency, he might." I look around the room for a friendly face.

Lydia gives me a small, encouraging arm squeeze. "Oz is in charge. If something goes wrong, they'll send for him right away."

A wicked gleam flashes over the mermaid's face. "I'm all for stealing the horn from that bastard, but we need a *good* diversion, not some stupid fight or injury. Oz would see right through that."

Flynn combs his blond hair back with one hand. "We need him out of his cabin for half an hour tops. Jules will let me in, and we'll steal the horn right under the dragon's nose."

Lydia glares at the littered floor. "How do you know your dimensional rings work on a Magisterium safe?"

"I've done it before. They work. But it will trip the safe's alarm."

We all exchange a glance.

Jeremy grumbles. "So, even if we manage to steal it, he'll just take it back."

"Not if it's gone," I say quickly.

Brie offers up both palms in surrender. "The beach is under strict surveillance. I can't smuggle anything or anyone out of here again."

I bite my bottom lip and wait for the silence to set in. The discouragement on each of their faces pushes me to share my dangerous idea. "There's a Faerie portal in Oz's cabin, the same one we used for the beach games. We could use it." I stretch the nerves out of my arms and wait for their reaction.

Lydia shakes her head. "Are you crazy? What are you going to do in Faerie?"

"We bring the horn to Cole, away from Oz." I force a steadying breath down my lungs. Flynn's nod of approval is enough to convince me that I've indeed lost my mind. "We can figure out the rest later."

"We could all get expelled," Jeremy whines.

"You? I already spent five days in an interrogation room this month. You're not even a footnote in this adventure, dog." Brie's lime-green hair starts to gleam. "But I have an idea for a diversion. Simple enough not to raise Oz's suspicions, but big enough to get his attention."

I shiver at the vindication in her eyes.

"The weather forecast announces a rise in humidity and temperature. There's a big thunderstorm coming. I say we set fire to the forest on the eastern cliffs. I can easily put it out after a few minutes."

Flynn grabs his chin. "That could work."

I open my mouth to disagree, but a loud bang on Jeremy's bedroom door steals my thoughts.

"Jules, open up," Trent shouts.

The proximity of his voice showers icy rain over our pyromaniac brainstorming, and we all turn a shade whiter. This isn't a joke. Are we really going to set fire to Dark Falls, even for a moment? What if Trent heard Brie's hypnotic voice through the door?

The doorknob rattles. "Jules, I know you're in there."

We all look at each other with wide eyes.

"He can't know we're all here. It's suspicious as hell," Brie hisses.

Lydia hides her face in her hands. "It's more suspicious if we don't answer."

"I'll get rid of him," I say.

Before I can move, Flynn strolls to the door and swings it open like he ordered pizza, smiling from ear to ear. "What's up, Darkwood?"

Brie and Lydia flatten their bodies to the wall to make themselves invisible from the doorway.

I walk past Jeremy to the front of the room.

Trent searches my gaze. "There is no way you're fucking this debauched Ken barbie-doll, so tell me the truth. What's going on?"

Flynn wraps an arm around my shoulder. "What is it to you, bloodsucker?"

Trent curls his fists over his black uniform pants. "Be careful, elf, or you'll soon rot in a cell."

The boys have brawled before, and the last thing I need is for them to attract any more attention, so I poke Flynn's side, hard enough to bruise him.

He doesn't acknowledge my efforts and puffs his chest instead. "Big words for a guy who hides inside his daddy's shadow."

Trent laughs, devoid of joy. "We can't all be unwanted little orphans like you."

Darkness flickers in Flynn's blue eyes, but his smile widens. When Flynn Verinos flashes you his signature smile, you know you're in for some pain. He might not dish it out now, but it's coming, and you know in your gut it's coming.

Trent inches back.

"At least, I can get laid without magic." Flynn prowls behind me and snakes his arms around my neck. One hand hangs casually between my breasts. "How's your sister? Has she forced herself on anyone else, yet?" His hot tongue dips in my ear, punctuating his question with a dash of scandal.

This cover doesn't feel even half-innocent anymore, and Flynn clearly indulges in more theatrics than necessary. He revels in the game.

Trent throws his jacket to the ground. "Let Jules go and face me like a man. I'm going to erase that stupid smile—"

Flynn bites my neck hard enough to draw blood. I wince at the pinch, but the sweet kiss he places there a second after liquefies my bones. Flynn is no vampire, but he hums at the taste anyway—pushing the boundaries of the tentative trust we'd been nurturing.

I draw in a deep breath not to blast him off me. He licks the wound clean. I tell myself it's to rattle Trent and draw him away, but I can't ignore the fiery blush on my cheeks.

The vampire's throat bobs, his sight riveted on my neck. "You let him bite you like that? Like it's nothing?" he scolds quietly, the words barely audible.

"Have fun playing with yourself, Darkwood." Flynn slams the door in Trent's face.

The loud thump resonates in my scrambled brain.

I slap Flynn's chest. "What the fuck?"

"He didn't believe we were a thing before." He shrugs without meeting my gaze. "He believes it now." He starts to move deeper into the room.

I grip his arm to block his escape. "Did you have to bite me? Fae don't care about blood."

Flynn's cerulean eyes pulse with shadows. "All immortals care about blood."

Brie drums her nails over her red lips but fails to cover up her bright smile. Her hair gleams with golden accents. "Especially you, Verinos." She rubs his shoulder blades over his shirt.

The Fae sidesteps fast enough for his heavy boots to scuff the carpet.

Brie snickers and braces her hands on her hips. "So, about my plan. Let's get into the nitty gritty."

What the hell was that about?

I tuck my chin in and ignore Lydia's knowing smirk. The redhead will not let me live this down.

I know nothing about Flynn, his life in Faerie, or his family. I figured he was the son of a high-ranked courtier or a wealthy trader. When I picture Cole and Flynn as children, I see two spoiled devils running around Faerie, wreaking havoc on the less fortunate and throwing rocks at mortals. Maybe that's a tad cliché and diminutive, and I wonder what else I missed.

WET LEAVES and the acrid smell of rot fill my lungs. Dew hangs in the early night air, the spring days running longer and longer. Chipmunks sprint in and out of their holes along the crooked path leading to Oz's cabin.

"You're late." Flynn joins me on the trail and falls into step with me. "Not looking forward to your date with the professor?"

A sigh escapes me. "I had to talk Jeremy through the whole plan again."

"He's jumpy. If tonight goes awry, we'll know who to blame." The washed-out gray Faerie clothes Flynn is wearing look soft to the touch. A carved dagger with silver and teal accents hangs from a belt at his side.

"What if the fire gets out of hand, and we hurt someone?" I rake my hands through my curls. I'm sure a few gray strands will grow after the night we had, trying to plan the perfect diversion to draw Oz out of his lair.

Brie's big idea to set fire to the forest was first discarded after Trent's interruption, but we circled back to it. She insisted that it would be easy to put out with her water magic, but I know how quickly a fire can get out of hand. Unfortunately, we couldn't find a better, more practical idea in so little time.

"If Oz is to leave you alone in his cabin with the unicorn horn, we need to create an emergency that doesn't strike him as something a student might do. Something that could happen naturally. Lydia's spell will ensure that the woods are empty and that the trees behind the line are protected from the fire."

"What about animals? Chipmunks for example?" I point to a little rodent skipping along a broken trunk next to us.

"You're worried about chipmunks right now? Oz summoned you to his cabin to talk about the trial. We're about to steal his most prized possession and run off to Faerie with it through a portal we're not even sure is still there. If I were you, I'd concentrate on that. Did you remember to eat one of Deveraux's cookies?"

"Of course! I'm not dumb enough to go to him without taking precautions. What about you? Why the knife?" I point to Flynn's side, trying to focus on anything else than our half-assed plan.

He unsheathes the weapon. The blade absorbs the ambient light, and a nefarious smog rises from it in waves like it was forged directly from shadows. "It's called an Obscurion. A dagger strong enough to kill a Fae."

"Why would you carry a weapon strong enough to be used against you?" Why would he carry a weapon at all? Magic is our thing, spells and orbs and illusions.

"Faerie's a treacherous place, especially with a newbie—a mortal, no less—in tow. Sprites and pixies are not the only ones with wings, claws, and teeth."

I click my tongue. He's probably yanking my chain for his own twisted entertainment. "You didn't carry a dagger for the beach games."

"Ah—a crafted illusion of peace, a well-guarded sanctuary to awe earthlings. That's not Faerie." Flynn stops as we draw near Oz's cabin. He rests one knee on the ground and laces up his knee-high boots. "You take your freedom—your safety—for granted. You could live a peaceful, privileged life in the human world, and yet you chose to attend the most dangerous school in the realm."

"You chose it, too."

His lopsided grin doesn't quite meet his eyes. "Given the choice between poison or death, is poison a choice at all?" He muses at his own question, chin angled to the sky. "If Jeremy does his job right, you have about fifteen minutes to spare. Use them wisely."

Pulling his dark hood over his platinum blond hair, he blends with the shadows once more and hides behind a large trunk.

My tongue sticks to the roof of my mouth, and I brace myself for what comes next. We arrived at the cabin from the east side, and I jump over a fallen tree to rejoin the main path. Fire flickers inside the cabin, its light visible through the large windows. Hands hidden in my hoodie's pockets, I walk toward the entrance.

Deep breaths. Here goes nothing. I knock on the thick wood and shift my balance from one foot to the other.

Oz's congenial voice blasts through the door. "Come in."

The hinges creak open. A metallic taste clogs my tongue, and within seconds, I'm floating on air. An aftertaste of jasmine and lilies lingers at the back of my mouth. Angel dust. I've read enough about the plant to know its signature taste. The bastard must have enchanted it to hang in the air so it would reach me when I walked in.

"Is everything alright?" Oz pats the space next to him on the blue velvet couch. "Come. Sit."

The compulsion to do as he asks is too strong to be ignored, and my legs obey of their own accord. My teeth grit together, and I force a sharp, painful breath down my lungs. The fresh gulp of air clears my foggy brain. Sweat pools at the back of my neck.

Oz's inquisitive gaze collides with mine. "Answer my question truthfully." The order scratches its long claws inside the ridges of my brain, but it's not undeniable.

Deveraux's cookies work, but I obey Oz and sit beside him, working hard to wipe the surprise and disgust from my face.

He blinks a few times. "Have you prepared what you're going to say for the trial?"

"No," I answer honestly.

"Do you trust me?" He tilts his head to the side. There's no fake smile or forced warmth in his manner. A sharp wit shines in his gray stare.

My breath catches, but I sit still with my hands braced on my thighs. "I trust you, professor."

"You're a fascinating woman, Julia." His gaze falls to my necklace, and he turns the emerald between his fingers. "How do you summon infernal magic?"

"I don't know," I lie.

"That's unfortunate. Do you believe Mr. Desirys murdered the unicorn?" He rushes over the last word.

"Yes."

He studies me for a moment.

My heart hammers in my chest. Can he tell that I'm lying? Should I engage with him more? Angel dust is supposed to lull me into compliance, but maybe I should act a bit more natural. I force my shoulders to relax and add, "Cole slept with my sister and killed Miss Eillis. I hate him."

Blood drains from the professor's face, and a trembling hand hovers over his brows. "I hate him, too."

His reaction spooks me. Either Oz is still acting and knows that I'm not under his thrall, or he's genuinely upset. He scoots closer.

I stop breathing. *Fuck no!*

But if I punch him, he'll know for sure that I'm not under his control.

He leans in until we share breath, and his eyes flick down to my lips. "Do you find me attractive?"

"Yes." Clearly, that's the only right answer.

"Do you want me to kiss you?"

Hell to the fucking never.

"I—I—" No matter how much I want to play along, my tongue refuses to utter anything but curses.

He cups my cheek. "You have fire inside you. Just like me."

Knots tug at my gut. It's just one kiss, but it costs me every ounce of self-control I possess not to recoil when Oz claims my mouth.

He thinks he's got me under his power. He could ask any question and hope to receive an honest answer, and yet seducing me, using me as a willing female, seems to be his one and only play. What kind of madness empowers him to behave this way? Isn't he content with all the sex he has with my sister? What kind of twisted ego boost does this bring him?

Squeezing my eyes shut, I think of anything else but Oz—his lips, or his wandering hands. I focus on the fact that I'm not under his thrall, but about to rob him. The thought pushes me to reciprocate the kiss instead of merely suffering it. I'll steal Oz's most-prized possession. If I could only see his expression when he realizes what I did...

He pulls back, breathless. "You're the rule breaker of the family. We're rebels, you and I." His attention turns to his signet ring. The Academy's insignia burns bright red on it. "Fuck! Why now?"

A note bursts into existence on the back of the couch, and Oz unfolds it quickly.

His gaze flies from the windows back to me. "Wait for me here. Do not move from this couch until I return, okay?"

I plaster a dreamy smile on my lips. "Okay."

His hot thumb glides across my cheek. "You will not remember this moment, but I do look forward to kissing you for the first time again."

With that, he barrels out of the cabin. The door thunders shut behind him, and I start to count to twenty inside my head.

When I reach nineteen, I gulp in a heavy, disgusted breath.

My hands tremble, but I shake off the slimy, oily memory of Oz's goodbye and wipe his manipulative kiss off my lips with the back of my hand.

I wrench open the cabin door and signal Flynn.

The tall Fae sneaks past the wards without setting them off. As expected, Oz left in a hurry and didn't bother to arm them properly. I'm not even sure he could have managed it with me still inside. I blow air out of my mouth. One thing about this stupid plan worked, at least. Flynn passes me my bag and dashes to the bedroom with a crowbar in his hands. To access the safe, he removes five or six pieces of hardwood. The display of grace and stamina quickens my heart, and I wish the Fae garments didn't enhance his angelic traits—or my pesky fascination with them.

We both kneel to peek at the blue metal box.

Chills scatter across my neck, and I grip Flynn's upper arm. "Wait. It's still here. The nether being Lydia and I saw the other night."

He pauses and searches the room. "That upside-down spell pulled a number on you. There's nothing here but you and me." Flynn twirls his right hand over the safe. His magic carves a temporary hole into the thick metal. A pristine, pearly-white horn lays inside. The sight of the severed end wrenches my insides.

Flynn's blue eyes flutter shut for an instant. With extreme care, he grabs the horn and wraps it in a dark piece of cloth. "Let's go."

We double back into the main room.

A black tarp covers the tall, old-fashioned mirror that doubles as a Faerie portal, and I tear off the fabric. "Where does it lead? To the beach like last time?"

Flynn shakes his head. "This is Oz's portal. It'll take us to where he went last."

Adrenaline chases the elation in my veins. "Isn't that a problem?"

The golden frame gleams in the night. Inside the mirror, I see myself as a Fae. The luscious black curls and heart-shaped mouth of this otherworldly beautiful Julia raise every single hair on my arms. I slip the cherry wood necklace I brought over my emerald pendant, hoping it'll protect me from the mind-numbing luster of Faerie.

"Last chance to turn back, mortal." Flynn offers me his hand, and I clasp it without thinking.

We both stare at our entwined fingers for too long.

Flynn stretches his arms and cracks his neck. "Don't worry, if an Unseelie attacks us, you will probably die quickly, given your constitution."

A dry chortle pops out of my mouth. "Is that supposed to make me feel better?"

"Yes. Being eaten sucks more when you're alive for most of it." With that horrific joke, Flynn pulls me into the glass.

I clasp the cherry wood necklace with my free hand and hold my breath.

9

THE DIM WARLOCK

Allie

" *T*he damn Fae put me out of service right when it counted." Olson Lewis slams his fist on the mattress. "I could have thwarted his plans."

A chilly wind flows into the private room of the infirmary, and I get up to close it. A half-crescent moon illuminates the night sky. "Just chill, Olson. You're lucky enough to be alive."

The warlock's hair has grown during his hospital stay, his usually polished half-buzz cut shaggier than usual. The roots of his blue hair betray the true color underneath—a dark, dirty brown that robs him of his edgy look.

Mouth dry, I consider his lean muscle mass and try to concentrate on anything but the fact that I'm responsible for his presence here. Daniel and I had to test the angel dust on Cole. It worked flawlessly, too, and the prince sent his demon cat after Olson without a hitch, as though it had been his own intention.

Olson's part to play was the damsel in distress, a role he played to perfection. He missed a few weeks of school, but he's alright. I return to sit by his bed. "I'm sure you'll be asked to testify at the trial. This isn't over."

"Yeah, you're right." His warm hand rests on top of mine. "I'm just glad you're okay."

The intimate gesture sets me on edge. I smack my lips together and jump to my feet. "Well, I have to go. Visiting hours are over."

"Won't you stay just a few more minutes?"

"You know I can't. Dr Chen is very strict. Goodnight." The doorknob clicks into place behind me. I close my eyes and lean against the door I just closed.

Olson is terrible at keeping secrets. What happens if he spills the beans to Jules about the love potion we prepared together?

The commotion that awaits me outside sparks electricity at my temples. Students gather on the cliff, and red hues light the night sky with fiery tints.

I run to the huddle and find Trent there.

"There's a fire in the forest." The vampire's ashen face wrinkles with fear.

I dig my nails into my left wrist. "Do you think it's Jules?"

"I don't know."

Was Jules angry and crazy enough to set fire to the forest? Pent-up emotions are known to set her—and her surroundings—ablaze.

Brie dashes to the edge of the cliff, her eyes red and black. "I got it." The mermaid raises her arms to the sky, and thunder answers her call as scales appear on her arms.

A salty mist drugs my senses. "Check Summer Hall," I tell Trent.

He nods gravely before running down the main path.

I pull my hoodie over my long, blond hair and retreat into the line of trees. Once hidden by a shroud of darkness, all eyes turned in the other direction, I let my magic build in my palms and rise into the air.

Humidity condenses on my cheeks, the barometric pressure wacky and unnatural, and a pesky wind threatens to blow me off course. My ankles skim the treetops as I fly, hell-bent on avoiding attention. Even under the current circumstances, elation sizzles through my blood.

Flying came naturally to me. Daniel taught me how to channel my magic, but even he was astonished by my speed and expertise.

Raindrops pound my arms in a rapid rhythm. As I get close to the fire, my heart accelerates.

Flames rage above the ancient cave at the foot of the mountain, and the heat expands the pores on my face. Mom took me there on my first day to explain the origins of the school and the legacy of our presence here. The tepid current of power that usually emanates from it ripples in sync with the flames. Dark Falls' darkest and deepest mystery pulses in trepidation like it's…excited about the fire. Like it can't wait for the whole forest to burn.

Just as I'm about to turn back, a deafening crack splits the air, and not from the clouds above, but from the earth below. The deep bedrock of the mountain rips in two under my frozen stare, and white fog slithers out of the stones. The strange shimmer dissolves quickly, but the smoke from the fire billows above the burning trees.

A line of liquid shadow glistens in mid-air, right above the rock slab. It beckons, but I know better than to blindly jam my finger into Dark Falls' power outlet.

The rain intensifies, so I land near the trail that leads back to the Academy to escape the icy kiss of the storm. Wet, cumbersome clothes stick to my skin.

I watch the trail for signs of life, knowing I shouldn't be found drenched to the bones near the fire, and swerve toward Daniel's cabin to check on him. The fire is on the opposite side, but he said he had an important meeting tonight and shouldn't be disturbed. Maybe he doesn't know what's going on.

As I near the cabin, a soft, strangled cry reaches my ears, and I search the forest for the source of the sound. A few paces to the left, Jeremy lies on his side among the ferns. I glance over my shoulders. I shouldn't be seen here, but his laments quicken my pulse. Had Cole's demon cat started to hunt on its own?

I approach slowly.

He whimpers, all curled up in a fetal position. A sheen of sweat shines over his tall forehead, and decomposed leaves pepper his bare chest.

I sprint through the last few steps and kneel at his side. "What happened to you?"

"There was s—something in the woods. I—Ice and a twinkle of light. It bit me—I think." Vicious shivers rock his body.

"Did you see what set the fire?" I observe the woods again, but as far as I can tell, we're alone. Magic prickles the nape of my neck. A restless current of energy still lurks in the air, but I can't pinpoint its origin. "Can you walk?"

He shakes his head with a wince.

I pat my empty pockets. I left my cell phone in my room, and I don't have a pen or paper to send a note. "I'll get help. Don't worry."

Fuck. Fuck. Fuck. Daniel will scream my head off for this. I'm supposed to lie low, not run to the Academy for help, but I can't leave Jeremy to die here. With shallow breaths, I bolt off to the dining hall.

RED THUNDER

Jules

The mirror spits us out inside a dark cellar. The icy kiss of inter-realm travel skitters along my back, quickly replaced by the stuffy, hot ambient air. Wooden planks screech under our weight, and Flynn presses his index finger to his mouth. With a grave nod, I hold my breath.

Wood barrels are stacked along the walls and marked with white chalk. Massive terracotta cooking pots clutter the counter space, but spiderwebs and dust seem to be the only things on the menu.

Faint voices and warm flickers of light echo into the cellar coming from the other side of the wall.

Flynn motions to the blackened window on the opposite wall. It's high up, close to the ceiling, but wide enough for us to squeeze through. Without a sound, he removes the pin lock, opens the glass pane, and secures it with a braided cotton thread hanging from the exposed wood beams.

"Mind your head." He laces his fingers to create a step.

I brace myself on his left shoulder as he boosts me up. A nasty splinter from the window frame buries into my thumb, but I tuck my arms and elbows in and crawl into the tall grass.

Faerie is so much...colors and movements and textures explode to life in a way that my mortal brain struggles to process. I hold out my hand to help Flynn. Once we're both safe out of the cellar, I climb to my feet.

Clouds rumble above our heads and spark a storm of butterflies in my stomach. The silver-flecked grass caresses my calves like an old lover. Beauty beckons from all sides—so close I could reach for it—starting with the Fae on my right.

"Fuck, we're in Thurst." Flynn's bright glamor glitches and fades. His honeyed skin melts down to a smooth, stony gray, and the lustrous golden accents of his hair vanish.

A wide dirt road separates us from a cozy, round hut. The sand-colored building clashes with the dark forest behind it. A narrow chimney splits the roof in two and embalms the air with the smoky, greasy promise of a fresh kill.

Flynn pulls the hood of his jacket over his head and molds his body to the brick wall at our backs. "We stick out like sore thumbs."

Sweat drips along my back. "What are you doing?"

He pulls two loose ponchos out of his bag. "This village is less than a day's walk from Unseelie territory. We can't be seen."

I slip on the gray, old-fashioned cotton poncho but leave the hood off. The grooves of the rough fabric scratch my skin. "Why would Oz come here?"

"Excellent question." Flynn guides me toward an old barn flanked by thick, unfamiliar conifers. "No Fae lives here, except crooks and thieves."

The purple needles of the trees shimmer with black and teal accents. I could spend a whole day marveling at the intricate, gnarly patterns created by their branches as they stretch to the sky, but I tear my gaze away and follow Flynn over the fence.

A majestic palomino percheron stomps at our approach. After a few seconds, he trots in our direction. While the scenery and plants are all Faerie, the beast looks as earthly as they come.

Flynn slowly raises his knuckles to its muzzle.

The magnificent horse sniffs the offered hand and shakes its head from side to side before it bows down, its blond mane dancing in the wind.

"It recognizes you," I say on a hunch.

Flynn slides open the barn door. "Not exactly. Fae and horses understand each other."

The hinges squeak in tune with a sharp crack of thunder. Crimson clouds roll in the sky, and thick, red-tinted water splashes on my arms. The heavy raindrops prickle my skin.

Lightning illuminates the bloody sky and echoes in every fiber of my soul. I could die here, watching the fury of the storm.

Flynn snaps his fingers in front of my face. "Shape up, mortal."

I shake off the urge to dance in Faerie rain and follow him.

He drags me to the back of the barn and boosts me up to the hay loft. "Quick, before someone sees us."

Graceful and meticulous as a cat, he jumps up after me and ushers me deeper inside the alcove. The door's hinges squeak again, and we hide behind a stack of hay.

The horse's owner tucks him in for the night. I steal a peek at the tall man through the planks. He's mortal, one of the humans who live in Faerie.

I watch him feed the horse, two little pigs, and a few chickens. I've never met a Faerie slave. His clothes are similar to Flynn's. Outdated by my standards, but well made and durable. He whistles a soft tune and hurries off.

After he's gone, Flynn passes me loose cotton pants and a pair of leather boots. "We'll leave in the morning. At the break of dawn, the market in town we'll be busy, and we can join the bustle without anyone being the wiser."

The space is cramped, but with a few adjustments, we could sleep here. "What if Oz chases us?"

A spark of Fae magic skitters in Flynn's palm. "He can try. This isn't the Academy. I'll gladly teach that dragon a lesson."

Despite his bravado, I'm nervous. Oz isn't a high-ranking Magisterium officer for nothing. "What about my powers? Am I weaker in Faerie?"

Flynn stares at me, all serious. "Are you strong somewhere?"

I slap his chest, and the warm inflections of his laugh ripple across my heated cheeks.

"Turn around while I put these on." I peel the nylons off my legs and discard the skirt in favor of Flynn's extra pair of pants. They're too big, but it's not uncomfortable. Same with the boots. They fall right below my knees and protect my skin from the chafe of the hay and wood.

While I change, Flynn picks a few apples from a tree snuggling the barn. Dimensional rings allow him access through the thin sheet of goffered metal, and the tree plies to meet his grip. He dries the apples off with his shirt and offers me one.

The luster of the peel beckons.

"Mortals aren't supposed to eat Faerie fruits," I say.

"You believe in fairytales, now?" Flynn teases.

I squint at him. "Should I?"

"'Faerie fruits' is a puritan euphemism for sex…the apples are harmless," he adds with a wink.

"You better not be yanking my chain." I nibble on the apple.

It tastes…more. Red, sweet and fresh and soft and comforting—my mortal taste buds can't get enough. I press the back of my hand to my mouth and hum before taking a full, unbridled bite.

Rain drums an uneven melody on the roof, but nothing leaks inside, so the structure must be sound. My eyes slowly adjust to the growing darkness.

I swallow another mouthful of the infuriatingly delicious apple. "Is your glamor off? Is that why your skin looks gray?"

He examines his arms and hands. "It's more like an ugly glamor. It takes me more energy to look this unappealing than to not."

Stifling a snort, I bite my tongue. He doesn't look *unappealing* at all.

Normal—yes. If it wasn't for the gray tint, I could believe he was human.

"What is Unseelie territory?" I ask.

"Faerie isn't all glitter and beauty. In the last decade, Unseelie attacks have crept closer and closer to the capital. They asserted control of a few villages that used to be ours, one of them close by."

"I thought Unseelie Fae were primitive?"

"You thought wrong. Sure, the majority of them aren't the most organized bunch, but they've been relentless the last few years. We're at war." He tosses the apple's core to the ground below, and our furry roommate neighs in thanks.

I raise a brow. "How come I never heard of this?"

"You think we're going to advertise our internal conflicts to earthlings? This war makes us vulnerable. How can we stay ahead of earthling politics when we're busy fighting Unseelie monsters at our borders?"

I inch closer. "If it's so dire, how come you don't have to fight?"

Flynn leans back on the hay with his hands braced beneath his head, his elbows stretched wide. "Oh, but I will. Mandatory military service awaits."

I shuffle some hay underneath my ass and build a pillow with my discarded clothes, keeping the poncho on. "I thought your life was all feasts and prostitutes."

"Feasts and prostitutes help you forget that your life isn't really your own."

The flippant logic coaxes a smile out of me, and I turn back to face him. The Fae nestles onto his side. From this angle, I can count the tiny freckles on his face.

The close quarters suddenly feel a bit claustrophobic, and I scoot away from him, putting as much space between us as possible.

He holds himself up on one elbow. "Are you afraid I'll snuggle you if it gets cold?"

I press my lips together to calm my frazzled heartbeats. "Maybe I snore."

A bright smile spreads on his lips, and he shifts onto his back again, one hand resting on his stomach. "I would expect nothing less from you, mortal. Nothing less."

FLEABAG

Jules

H ay stuck to my palms, I wake with a start. The rhythmic breathing of the horse is gone. Adrenaline rushes through my blood, but I can't put a finger on what woke me from the dreamless sleep.

Dry bedding crunches under my weight as I shift to my side. Darkness blinds me completely. The torrential rain from before gave way to a quiet drizzle, and the temperature has dropped significantly.

With a deep sigh, I press on my beating heart, willing it to return to a normal rhythm, until a clicking sound tickles my ears. The *tick-tick-tick* reminds me of a cockroach skittering across the floor.

I shiver at the thought of Faerie insects and what they might look like.

"Flynn?" I paw at the darkness. The space beside me is empty, and my throat bobs. "Stop toying with me."

Goosebumps prickle my neck. "Flynn!"

No answer.

I push my fire forward to pierce the night. Flynn's body left a deep imprint in the hay, but the Fae is gone. A whiff of night air blows past my legs. A cold cackle rumbles across the metallic sheets covering the barn. It creeps closer and closer until I hear a voice in my head.

Oh my! Can it be? An earthling has come to fill my belly?

A sting in the tender flesh of my arm burns enough for me to cry out in surprise. Before I can move, a languid, insidious lull takes hold of my body. My muscles melt from the inside out. I'm paralyzed.

Eyes wide, I search for the source of the heart-wrenching clicks, each of them echoing deep in my soul like a butcher's knife against bone. Rain trickles along the roof.

Death? Failure? What dreary future gnaws at your delicious, quickened heart? To be eaten alive, perhaps, or paralyzed?

"Show yourself," I croak.

A greyish, human-shaped hand closes around my calf, but I can't move—a frozen statue imbued by fear.

My belly cramps.

Ohh—I see. I see what you fear, earthling.

Long black nails scratch my skin, and a shudder of revulsion rattles me to my core. Fireballs burst from my limp hands, and I manage to blast the creature, but it barely twitches in response.

To be irrelevant. To be forgotten. You fear your own mortality. He hehehe.

The creature chucks out a high, distorted giggle, and I catch a glimpse of its terrible features. It's got the build of a lanky teenage girl, the round cheeks of a doll, big eyes, and a hairless head.

No one escapes the skin they were born in. No one but me. Let me wear your skin, earthling. Let me taste your destiny.

It cocks its head, more insect than human.

I refrain from blinking not to miss a movement, desperately pushing my magic forward.

A blade slices the night, and the monster screeches and skitters out of view. Its clicks become quick and impatient.

Two for one. How interesting.

A Seelie and his lover, perhaps?

Flynn's Obscurion finds nothing but shadows. The blue-tinged knife gleams in the darkness.

"Unseelie scum. I'll gut you myself." Flynn scours the pitch-black space for his enemy, his knees bent, and his arms spread out, ready to strike.

Yes. You were meant to die together. Your fears are so deliciously similar.

Screwing my lids shut, I concentrate on my breathing and summon Beth's advice from my memory. Inhale. Exhale. Slice the creature in two like the apple and the banana. I'd practiced my infernal orbs again a handful of times since that night with Onyx and cut down quite a few trees. It should be easy, but fear almost consumes me as the Unseelie sinks its long nails into Flynn's back and sends him flying head-first into the hay bales.

He howls in pain. The Unseelie latches onto him and licks the fresh wound. A hum of unadulterated pleasure gurgles through the hayloft as it chews on a piece of Flynn's flesh.

My blood stills.

I'll peel you slowly, Seelie boy. One strip at a time.

The monster munches on Flynn like he's nothing more than a bag of chips, and I explode into a fury of purple sparks. My magic claws its way across the wood planks. I ram the creature with it, praying to the Dark Gods that it doesn't kill Flynn in the process.

With a sickening crunch, the Unseelie falls over the edge of our hideout to the ground below, split down the middle.

The wave of paralysis lifts instantly. Our horse friend below neighs and stomps, suddenly agitated, and I sigh in relief—I thought it might be dead.

"Where did it go?" Flynn wobbles to his feet and examines the walls and ceiling like he expects the Unseelie to dart out of the cracks at any moment.

I light the barn with a fresh ball of fire and check the corpse again. "It's dead."

"Dead?" He throws his knife from one hand to the other.

I point to the floor below us. "Yes. What was it?"

With a heavy breath, Flynn sheathes his weapon. "A peeling hag." He reaches helplessly for his back.

Drenched with blood and ripped to shreds, his shirt does little to hide the extent of his injuries, but none of them are life-threatening—not for an immortal Fae. A whip would have left a cleaner mess, though. I grip the black nails embedded deep in his flesh and pull them out.

Fists balled at his sides, Flynn sinks to his knees in the hay. "Ow. Careful. I feel like my nerves have been dunked in acid."

"Fire didn't work, so I used infernal magic. It sort of got away from me."

The intensity of his stare sparks goosebumps on my skin. "Let's be real, your fire magic could barely cook a meal. I thought you'd just juiced up on infernal magic, appealed to some dark patron for a fix to beat Cole and attract attention. I didn't know you had it *inside* you."

Shit. Flynn doesn't know I'm half-demon, and while I'm relieved that Cole hasn't spilled the beans, I want to keep my secret. "It's no big deal."

"It's a fucking big deal. You killed an Unseelie *with your powers.*"

I roll my eyes, trying to make light of it. "And you think I'm weak, I get it."

He shows off his knife. "This metal is the *only* weapon that works against them. They are incredibly resistant to magic. If you've got enough infernal magic in you to kill an Unseelie..."

I scoff. "I'm sure someone used infernal magic on them many times before."

"It's not an incredibly popular strain of magic." He checks his arm and winces at a nasty cut in his left bicep. "You almost ripped my arm off."

I press my old Academy shirt to the wound. "Sorry about that."

"Don't be. It's a nick compared to the ones on my back." He applies pressure to the gash and motions to his bag. "I have some healing cream in there somewhere."

Kneeling, I unclasp the leather belt of the small satchel. Flynn used a spell to enlarge the interior, and I catch a glimpse of the Fae stela. He clearly doesn't expect to go back to Dark Falls anytime soon. I find the tube of healing cream, uncork the top, and squeeze it.

A sprout of pasty cream oozes into my hand. "You used me as bait."

He scratches the back of his pointy ear with his free hand. "Hey, I didn't have much of a choice."

I mutter the correct incantation and apply a thin coat of cream to the cut on his upper arm. The magic leaves a fresh patch of skin in its wake. I move to his back, and the damage there is so extensive that my eyes struggle not to screw shut at the sight of the gooey, burgundy clumps of blood.

I don't have a weak stomach by any means. I've seen my share of injuries these last few months, but Flynn's usually perfect skin is in shambles, and a big chunk of flesh is missing.

He shifts forward and braces his arms around a bale of hay, his biceps straining. "I'm ready. Do it." Sweat pearls on his neck. "Don't bother to do a perfect job. Unseelie claws leave a permanent mark. Always."

With a grave nod, I peel the shredded shirt off his back. There can't be any foreign bodies for the healing cream to work its magic, but a few pieces of cloth are stuck inside the wound.

Lips pressed together, Flynn rests his forehead on the hay, his arms shaking. "You're quite the nurse, Winslow." He fails to hold in a scream as I pick off the last piece. "Remind me never to turn my back on an Unseelie again—not even to save your life."

A smile plays at the corners of my lips. "If I remember correctly, I saved *you*," I tease, hoping it'll distract him from the pain.

"Hey! If I hadn't sensed the hag's arrival and attacked it, buying you time to build your dark mojo, you would be a filet-o-witch by now. We saved each other."

"Totally. We saved each other." I nod with exaggerated enthusiasm and apply a thick coat of healing cream to his back, trying to ignore the bile in my mouth. Fresh skin seals the gash after a minute, and I breathe a little easier.

"You don't have to be so cocky about it," he mumbles grumpily.

"And you don't have to be such a guy." With a chuckle, I check to make sure I didn't miss a spot.

Two parallel, vertical, silver lines topped with a bite mark now stand where the deep, messy wound used to be. By chance—or twisted Fae design—the remnants of the attack run from Flynn's shoulder blades down the length of his spine before they disappear below his belt, drawing attention to his ass.

I let my fire orb burn out and pat his shoulder. "There. Good as new. Your next conquests will rave about your sexy scars."

Rain barrels above our heads, and in the dim light, I see Flynn's answering smile.

INSTEAD OF A BUSTLING MARKET, sunrise gives way to loud, heartbreaking laments. Flynn returns from the village with a big frown on his face. "Unseelies breached the walls last night and killed five mortals."

He slips a few fresh apples in his bag. "We need to create as much distance between us and Unseelie territory as possible. A pair of Fae travelling together attracts less attention than the two of us, so wear your hood."

The fabric sparks static electricity in my hair as I pull the hood over my head. "You think I can pass as Fae?"

"No, but if they don't see your face, maybe we'll get lucky."

I stick my tongue out at him, and he laughs.

We slip out of the barn before the owner returns to feed the animals.

Flynn's boots send dirt into the air as he sets a quick pace. "The next village is bigger and well-traveled. Once we get there, I'll buy two horses, and we can ride until dusk. We'll have to camp out in the woods to avoid attention, but at least we can travel faster than on foot."

"You have enough money to buy horses?"

"I do now." He holds his bag open to show me his treasure. "We should be in Mellen in two days."

According to Flynn, all the Faerie roads lead to Mellen, the capital city.

The city where Cole is supposed to be. Flynn couldn't use his stela to coordinate our efforts since our plan came together at the last minute, but the thought still quickens my breath.

The Seelie Court. That'll be interesting to see.

"Cole mentioned the different Faerie time zones. How do we keep track of how much time has passed at the Academy?" A shiver runs through me. Two days until I see Cole again...

Flynn pulls a pocket watch from his trousers and clicks it open. "This watch was enchanted to always show the same date and time as the Dark Falls library. It's only ten pm for them, so we've been gone for less than two hours. Thurst has been stuck in a mild *ahtavar* current for years."

Cole had explained the specifics of Fae time zones minutes before we had sex, so my recollection of the terminology is messy. "*Mehjlirno* pockets are the ones that suck you in, and *ahtavar* currents are the ones that give you eons of time to make it home for dinner?" I sum up.

Flynn nods. "We call them M-pockets and A-currents. Time flows differently in all regions of Faerie, like the weather differs in your realm."

A sting behind my eyes announces the start of a headache. "How do Faerie folks keep track of it all?"

"We don't, really. We're immortal. Inter-realm travellers are a minority."

Chills run up and down my spine. "And the mortals?"

"We have two suns and five moons, so calculations can be done. Some particularly intense M-pockets are tracked on the royal maps. Mortal families mostly travel together to avoid cross-aging, but they're used to it. It's not uncommon for a father and his sons to look the same age if they chose to separate at one point."

"Ugh. Freaky."

If Oz has friends in this part, we manage to avoid them because our walk to the next village is uninterrupted.

Like Flynn predicted, the town is busier. Mortals, sprites, and pixies haggle over cluttered tables in the market.

An inn with a steep brass roof and colored glass panes comes into view. Above the wooden door, the detailed carving of an eagle stands with a horseshoe in its talons. A small hedgedog—a dog-shaped creature with black and yellow spikes—barks at our approach.

I'm more accustomed to the textures and colors by now, but I've only seen these creatures in textbooks.

Flynn walks past the main entrance of the inn and heads straight for the stables in the back. A mortal stable boy is pouring water in a wide trough, and the bucket in his hands shakes when Flynn steps closer, water spraying the ground.

The boy is tall but slim, with no real muscles to speak of, and he moves a bit awkwardly the way teens do when they are still getting used to their growing bodies.

"Can I help you, sir?" He keeps his gaze on the ground as he addresses Flynn.

The Fae presses a purse full of coins on the boy's chest. "I want two good, reliable horses, ready to go."

"Right away, sir." He almost trips over himself but hurries off.

He comes back fifteen minutes later with a fifteen-hands bay mare and a taller, dapple-gray gelding. Both horses are saddled.

Flynn pats the gray horse's neck and murmurs a few words. The horses' ears twitch and tip forward.

I turn my attention to the mare.

She looks at me with her big, soulful eyes. A heavy nicker rumbles through her lips.

"Hi," I say. Without thought, I grab the pommel and swing my right leg over the horse's back.

Flynn gawks, hands cramped over the reins. "You've ridden before."

"Wouldn't you like to know." I tap the horse's sides with my heels and ride off, keeping a slow pace until we pass the gates, then accelerate to a rhythmic trot.

My chest expands. It's been too long since I've ridden.

Flynn catches up to me, his movements fluid, and I've got no doubts he's used to this, too.

About an hour later, Flynn removes his hood, and his glamor starts to shine again. I guess his Seelie Fae-ness is no longer a liability.

The two Faerie suns, one orange and one red, slowly descend in the sky. The flow of time, weather, and daylight are things Faerie folks cannot take for granted. Flynn doesn't seem fazed by the growing darkness, but the horses slow down.

"Where did you learn to ride like that?" he asks.

His clear, friendly gaze warms my ears.

"Woodside, California."

Colorful crops flank the road on each side. Wheat, tobacco, and canola plants bristle in the wind.

"California is where all that Hollywood stuff takes place, right?"

I nod.

He huffs. "Humans. After beheading most of their kings and queens, they created new ones to worship."

He's not half-wrong. "Why is there no electricity in Faerie? Rumors have it that the Fae chose to keep the realm stuck in the Middle Ages to enforce their hold on the mortals."

The gelding falls in step with my horse.

"How do you expect electricity to behave in a place where even time glitches out of control?"

I nod in understanding. The gossip I heard growing up—like so many things I've heard about Faerie—was a twisted, vilified version of the truth.

"A life without technology must sound unappealing to you, but for us, it's the norm," Flynn says with an edge of dreaminess.

"It's not all bad." I point to the sky. "I've never seen so many stars before. It's beautiful."

Flynn closes his eyes and draws in a long, delighted breath. "It's home."

12

UNIFORMS AND COURTESANS

Jules

Mellen, the infamous capital of Faerie, is tucked between steep cliffs and the open sea. Dust blows over the winding road leading to the capital's gates. Hooves clank along the well-traveled path in a comforting beat.

The last two days passed in a blur. We stopped to rest a few times and shared the Fae equivalent of protein bars. According to Flynn's watch, the time "zone" switched on us again, and hours pass here about as fast as they do in Dark Falls, though, in their timeline, we've only been missing for sixteen hours.

The blond Fae points to the top of the cliffs in the distance. "There's the palace."

Blue and gold turrets gleam under the red sunlight, and my heart hammers at the grandeur and beauty of it. Carved directly into the mountain, the palace towers above the city. Deadly waves crash at its feet below.

Goosebumps tighten the skin of my arms as we pass the guards, their armors made of some unknown, yellow-tinted metal. Groups of mortals gallop, walk, or wheel past us. Sprites and pixies flap their leathery wings up and down sandy hive-like buildings. The air possesses the same salty and fresh quality I have grown accustomed to at the Academy, and I draw in deep, soothing breaths.

The path slowly ascends, and Flynn stops at an inn similar to the one where we bought the horses. "We'll hike the rest of the way to avoid attention. We can get the horses later."

I pat the mare's neck. "Thank you."

She neighs.

Flynn pays the horses' boarding fees to the innkeeper and pulls me along to a tiny staircase chiseled into the rock. "This is a shortcut. Keep your chin down, and don't meet anyone's gaze."

The climb is steep and tiring. Molten air weighs heavily on my shoulders. My calves scream from the abuse, the chafe of the leather boots throbbing on my big toe. Sweat drips down the valley between my breasts, and by the time we reach the top, Flynn's shirt is soaked through. He guides me through a maze of narrow alleys. "The royal servants live here with their families."

He opens a wooden door built into the rock wall, and we navigate a steep, uphill tunnel before we emerge in an interior courtyard where palm trees stretch toward the pink-tinged sky. A cloud of steam envelops me.

I wet my lips and taste the acidic, lemony-mist. "Where are we? Where is everyone?"

Flynn pushes me past the thick fog to the fountain in the middle. The square-shaped, open-roofed atrium is surrounded by windowless buildings. White, red, green, blue, yellow, and pink uniforms hang above our heads. Most of them are scandalous, no doubt used by the mortal courtesans Flynn always raved about.

He unclips a white tunic and matching pants from one of the clothing lines. "The royal laundry is washed and dried here. If I'm supposed to sneak us both inside the palace, we have to change."

I grab a similar uniform, but he points to the skimpy ones.

"Never." I brace my hands on my hips and swallow another mouthful of what I can only assume is a mix of detergent and perfume.

"May I remind you that we are both on the run? If you wear this, no one will question us." Flynn wades to the center of the fountain, the water coming up to his knees. Without an ounce of hesitation, he strips and runs his head underneath a water jet, rubbing his neck and shoulders.

His silver scars twinkle in the sun. They direct my gaze down the length of his back to his perfectly toned ass, like deviously well-placed flight attendants.

A wave of heat worse than all the ones I suffered through on our way over engulfs me, and I gawk. Back in the hay loft, I managed to touch his un-mangled back without issue, but now... I shield myself from the outrageous sight with one hand, but only manage to grip my curls and bite my lips.

He spins around, and flames turn my hot skin into lava.

Crystal-clear Fae water drips down Flynn's inked chest, and my total and complete inability to stop staring makes me question the efficiency of the cherry wood necklace around my neck.

He claps forcefully. "Stop ogling and get changed. Chop. Chop."

I force myself to turn around. "Did you have to strip?"

"I'm not entering the palace smelling like a gnome's butt, thank you very much. Besides, they won't let us in if we're filthy."

Flynn and Cole were supposedly attached at the hip growing up. Didn't he come to the palace often as a kid? From the corner of my eyes, I see him hop out of the fountain.

Flynn rubs a cloth to his head. "Hurry up. I know most of the servants that work here, but I'd still prefer to steer clear of them."

"I thought we would be safe in the city."

He wrangles a pair of lace-up pants past his knees and ties them below his bare abs. "We'll be safer with Cole, in the palace. Do you realize what we're carrying?" He swipes the horn from the bag, shoves it into his boot, and hides the rest of our stuff inside a dusty hamper.

With a grunt, I pry a blue courtesan outfit from the folded pile.

"Wear the black," Flynn says.

My eyes search for black, but I can't find any and arch a brow. "Does it matter?"

Flynn beelines for a thick chest in the corner and rummages through it for a minute. With a victorious grunt, he yanks out an identical uniform to the one I found, but in black.

"Why the fuck does it matter which color I wear?"

"It's Cole's color. We wouldn't want you to be summoned by another royal on our way in, now, would we?" Flynn grins from ear to ear like the prospect is hilarious.

I snatch the clothes from his hands. "How do I know it isn't your color?"

Flynn presses his lips together in a thin line. "If I had a color, you'd know."

My eyes skim the laundry. "Turn around."

Flynn spins to face the wall.

"Why do they use different colors, anyway?" I peel off my filthy clothes, and my heart squeezes as I unhook my bra.

"It makes it clearer which royal you want to fuck. White is for sharing."

"Ugh." I step into the fountain, and my muscles sing at the soft caress of water. I wet my hair too, scrubbing the sweat and dust from my body. "How many colors are there?"

"I will gladly draw you the Desirys family tree when we're not *tres-passing*." He turns around and hands out a drying cloth without stealing a peek, his gaze firmly glued to the side.

"You're awfully serious in Faerie."

The black top of the courtesan's uniform has sleeves, but it molds to my curves like a second skin. The roundness of my breasts stretches the soft satin. I tie a knot below my chest in a big bow and shimmy into the flowy, semi-translucent skirt. The fabric scratches my skin, and the train is long and bothersome. The design leaves my stomach bare, and I clutch the waistband of the skirt nervously. "Alright. I'm decent."

Flynn's blue eyes grow a shade darker, and I wait for him to mock me, but he carefully pries the necklace from my neck instead. "You can't wear the cherry-wood in the palace. That'd be like wearing gold to a goblin's wedding."

A shiver runs through me. "What's to stop them—or you—from lulling me into eternal servitude?"

Flynn skims my wet curls with his hand. "And we've got to do something about your hair."

"My hair?"

"It's too wild for the castle. Spin around."

I obey, and Flynn untangles the knots gently. When he separates it in three different strands and starts braiding, I gulp.

"You know how to braid hair?"

"I have four sisters." He works quickly and efficiently, adding hair to each twist. "What's up with your hair anyway? I'm certain you didn't have this purple lock yesterday." He dangles the end of a purple curl in front of my face.

I paw at my head. "That's new. I usually only get red ones. Is it big?"

"It's not discrete. Hopefully, the guards will think that you're trying to look like a Fae—not some magic weirdo who changes color overnight like a mood-ring." He laughs at the last part, pleased with himself.

A shaky breath flies out of my lungs. "How come we have to do all of this? Can't you just explain to the guards who we are? I mean—they don't know me—but you're Cole's friend."

"The Seelie court doesn't care much for friendship, just power and pedigree—and I have none." He tugs a little too hard. "I'm no one, okay?"

I press my lips together.

"I'm nothing. I'm a peasant who lucked out." He works my wild mane into a thick braid that falls over my shoulder to my front and ties the end with a golden ribbon. "The Academy only had space for one regular bloke like me because of the new policies. Talented Fae were turned down because of you, your sister, and the other mortals."

I pat down the flawless braid, shaken by his soft touch and angry words. "I'm no less worthy of an education than your Fae friends because I won't live as long. Fae might have a better affinity for magic than mortals, but talent can be found in many places."

"These Fae will fight the Unseelie without the elite training that could have spared their lives. Do you know how many of us die each year?" His voice cracks.

In the soft tremble of his voice, I detect a hint of grief. "You lost someone in the war."

"My father, but he wasn't exactly Dad of the year," he says, failing to hide a sniffle.

"I'm sorry for your loss." The nape of my neck tightens into goose-bumps as I entwine our fingers.

These last, wild days in Faerie blew me away. Flynn blew me away.

Gone is the savage, cruel bully I used to know, and the memory of him is not enough to tame my heart into submission.

He squeezes my hand, and I place a soft, chaste kiss on his lips.

He freezes—his entire body still, not breathing.

My lids flutter, but his remain closed, a marble statue of the David in front of me. The immobility unnerves me, so I press my lips to his again.

"Wow, you're useless without the cherry wood," he sighs.

Am I kissing him because of the compulsion of Fae magic? I think he's just too stunned to contemplate the alternative.

A shudder quakes through him as I trace the black tattoos on his chest, the ink visible through his sheer white shirt.

"What do they mean?" I ask.

His lips quirk up, but he doesn't answer.

Instead, he pinches the end of my braid. "Come on mortal, let's take you to your prince."

13

AUDIENCE

Jules

The hallways of the Seelie palace are paved with checkered tiles. Autumn-themed, metallic leaves form a limitless mosaic on the walls. Rows and rows of windows brighten both sides of a large drawing room where dozens of courtiers enjoy a respite from the harsh, midday heat, most of them oblivious to our presence.

Platters of fresh fruits, fragrant cheeses, and bubbly wines are being passed around by mortal servants in blue livery. Fae women in lavish gowns refresh themselves with wide decorative fans, each of them displaying mesmerizing textures and patterns. Glittering powders highlight their chiseled cheekbones and high brows.

My chest heaves. The black satin strains against my cleavage, and a hard band forms in my belly, but we mesh in well with the courtiers, and the guards pay us no mind.

Mortals live in farms and villages while the Fae gobble cakes and paint their faces...The frugal lifestyle I witnessed on our way here came straight from medieval times.

Disparities exist in the mortal world, but Faerie is on a different level. A sting of jealousy stretches to life in my blood. So much opulence and waste. So much beauty. So much time to sample an endless menu of pleasures and delicacies while the mortals work their fingers bloody to keep a roof over their heads. Not slaves, according to Cole, but do they truly have a choice?

Flynn guides me away from the crowd through a garden peppered with human-sized statues of embracing couples. There are no fig leaves to cover the men's...ample crotches. Statues in the Vatican didn't have them before the Renaissance, but the *loudness* of the pieces still shocks me.

The guards at the entrance let us pass without a second glance, but as we stride deeper and deeper into the palace, we see fewer servants and courtiers.

Copper and brass threads adorn the windows, entwined to form beautiful, eerie trees that stretch as high as the ceiling. The decorations cast hypnotic shadows on the ground, as if the forged forest lives and breathes, coming alive with each step we take.

The long hallway leads to a thick, gold-plated door flanked by a nasty-looking sprite. The guard holds up his sword at our approach.

"I demand an audience with the prince," Flynn announces.

Blinding light reverberates off his smooth skin, the Fae glamor on full display, his fresh white cotton shirt molding to his upper body like a very snug glove.

The sprite appraises Flynn, then me, as though he's gauging our beauty to judge whether or not we are worthy. After a few seconds, he turns up his bony nose, and the wings at his back twitch. "The prince is not receiving visitors at the moment."

We haven't made it as far as the entrance to the throne room only to turn back now. Magic skitters over my heated skin, and I almost blast the guard out of our way.

Flynn smirks. "The prince himself asked me to bring his new favorite to court. You will not deprive him of her company, will you?"

The soldier tilts his head to the side, his brows furrowed like he's only now seeing the black fabric barely covering my body. "Proceed." The lewd gaze crawls over my skin. To him, I'm nothing but fuckable eye candy.

Thick gold panels swing open quietly, and I freeze, my right hand flat on the doorframe. Shiny golden patterns embossed in the wood prickle my fingers.

In front of me, a narrow, carpeted runway leads to an altar where a dark Fae stretches over a chaise lounge. Two courtesans dressed in white hover around him. One of them—an older man—refills his cup while the other—a young woman—massages his feet.

Dazzles of Fae magic radiate from the metal crown on top of the Fae's head, the same colors as his earrings. Brass, copper, and silver nuances glimmer across his dark curls.

A black embroidered jacket highlights his large shoulders. Apparently sewn from the night sky itself, it sucks the light around him into the deepest and darkest abyss. The fabric shimmers with a nefarious energy.

Two burly men in uniforms stand at the back of the room, each of them holding a heavy sword.

Back at the Academy, his title always sounded a bit silly and self-aggrandizing, but here...

He's the prince of Faerie.

Fae magic smothers me from all sides. Eyes on fire and spine ablaze, I choke on the wretched taste of my mortality—my commonness. The sting of Cole's beauty grates my gut.

A Fae woman with a blood-red halter top and a bare stomach whispers something in the prince's ear. A diamond tiara sits on top of her head.

Flynn walks up to the front of the room in long strides and kneels before them solemnly.

There are several other people dispersed across the room. A stuffy looking sprite and a pink-glittered pixie glance in my direction, but I'm stuck in place. What am I doing here? My breath catches in my throat, and I cannot bear to look at Cole, or the woman next to him, or even the mortal slaves at his command.

Nails digging into the golden accents of the doorframe, I avert my gaze obstinately to the ground.

The guard standing next to me snarls. "Will you not greet your prince?"

My nostrils flare, but I stagger forward until I reach Flynn.

"Kneel," he whispers quickly.

I obey his command, bound by my promise.

I cannot for the life of me bring myself to look up at Cole, but I peek at his companion.

The red Fae scratches the armrest of her seat with her long, pointy nails. "Have you chosen a favorite, brother?"

A vicious cramp in my stomach dizzies me. I'm no one and nothing here. This was a mistake.

Cole stands, moving with considered carefulness and grace. My cheeks burn hot with disappointment. I don't know what kind of welcome I expected, but it wasn't this.

My soul screams. This place is the antithesis of everything I stand for. This elitist palace disgusts me, and I struggle to reconcile the not-so-secret excitement I nurtured about finally seeing Cole again with the reality of this stiff and pompous reunion.

His feet are bare, and I follow the familiar shape of his legs up to his sculpted chest and past his squared shoulders. Blue accents glisten on his skin, and red freckles shine in his amber eyes. The glass ceiling above us somehow directs all its light onto him. The colors swirl inside my mortal brain in a vertiginous dance.

He was already a lot to take in back home, but here, unmuted, untainted by my world, and surrounded by the power given to him by his birthright, he no longer appears human. He's not the man I fought against. He's not the mischievous teammate I studied with in the library, the evil ninja gravedigger, or even the vicious owner of a demon familiar.

I do not recognize this version of him, and it scares me to my core. A sickly sheen of sweat gathers on my palms.

"Leave us," Cole commands. The dark inflections of his voice burrow in every cell of my body.

The slaves on either side of him throw me jealous looks. Everyone that was present in the room before our arrival leaves, except Cole's sister.

"I can't wait to hear this." She chuckles like this is all some kind of live entertainment.

"Helena, this is Flynn Verinos," Cole says.

She licks her crisp, red lips and stretches to her feet, each move perfectly choreographed. "It's the mortal that interests me." She glides down the altar one step at a time and angles my chin up with the back of her index finger.

Humiliation simmers at the back of my throat.

"Jolie." The hypnotic chime sparks an itch on my neck. She releases me and angles her flawless body to Cole. "Bring them to your quarters. You have about an hour before Mother finds out."

14

LABYRINTH

Jules

Glossy floors melt into one another, tears blurring my vision. When we pass a brass, copper, and silver sigil, Flynn slows down his frantic pace. Cole dashes for a door that's half-hidden by the expansive decorations on the wall and ushers me inside a secluded, round stairwell.

The staircase runs many floors up and down, but it's clearly meant for the staff. Small torches burn along the gray walls at regular intervals to make up for the lack of windows. Spiderwebs weave around the flickering flames, and the acrid smell of mold grate my nose.

Flynn closes the door behind us and pries the unicorn horn from his boot. "We need to safeguard this."

Cole squeezes his shoulder. "Go downstairs and fetch Mary." Flynn spins around to leave, but the prince grips his elbow. "Thank you, Verinos. I won't forget this."

Their foreheads rest on one another for a split second.

Flynn acknowledges the praise with a quick tilt of the head before he hurries down the spiral.

Cole clasps my hand and yanks me in the opposite direction. At the top of the stairs, the passage opens to what I can only assume is his bedroom. His eyes rove my body from head to toe. The expression on his face confirms my worst fears.

"You look…" he trails off.

My fingers cramp around the long skirt. "I need to change out of this."

I might be a walking fantasy, but the hunger in his eyes isn't enough to soften my revulsion toward the clothes.

A bed towers in the middle of the room—twice the size of a king—and clearly meant for more than two people at a time. Rows and rows of books are tucked into the built-in design of the headboard. A series of windows offers a jaw-dropping view of the city.

The wretched aftertaste of magic in my mouth is too potent for me to think straight, and I'm 95% sure I got hit by a spell while I was in the throne room.

Cole grabs the knot between my breasts and wrenches me to him. "I'll help you change."

He digs his fingers into my waist, but I press hard on his chest. "Cole. Stop." My eyes remain glued to the floor, because I still can't bear to look at him. A heavy lump solidifies in my belly.

Cole skims my bare stomach before letting his hands fall at his side.

Allie's cruel jab echoes in my heart. *A Fae prince might want to fuck you now…*

I cannot give Cole the passionate reunion he so clearly desires. With a shaky hand, I grab my throat.

"Look at me." Cole reaches for my hand. "Jules, look at me."

I finally obey. He's standing inches from me, far enough to give me a bit of space, but close enough not to leave me exposed. From this angle, he looks a bit more like the Cole I used to know. I wish his familiar dimple was deep enough to bury all my ghosts.

He presses my palm flat over his heart. "Feel that rhythm?" His heart beats furiously beneath my fingers. "It's all you. I've plotted ways to break into Dark Falls and researched spells to draw you here. I've been…drunk with thoughts of you."

He cradles the side of my face. "Let's get you out of these stupid clothes." He arches a brow, waiting for my answer.

A minute ago, I felt empty. Insignificant.

I loathe the Fae for their customs and snobbery. I despise that their magic makes me question my self-worth. I hate how Cole transforms my mood with one lazy smile.

My throat bobs, but I nod and close the distance between us. Cole's taste—peaches and wine—knocks me back to reality, eroding whatever spell affected me before. He dismantles the satin knot and tosses the ribbon aside with a flick of the wrist. Flames rise from my skin to ravage what's left of the uniform. The embers crumble at our feet.

Cole's pupils dilate into two bottomless pools. The undertow of his next kiss causes me to stagger backwards, and my feet struggle to keep me standing.

He caresses a sweet, treacherous spot at the nape of my neck.

"I missed you," I whisper, the words so foreign and yet so right.

He grazes my shoulder with his teeth.

My doubts, my fears…the demons that reared their heads and chased us inside this room have vanished. Nothing else matters.

Cole fumbles with the intricate buttons of his jacket and shrugs it off. I stretch the neckline of his undershirt and wrangle it past his head. The smooth skin beneath gives me pause—sun-kissed by a different sun. A Faerie sun. The unearthly tan gleams, interrupted only by his tattoos. The black ink undulates like a liquid, bottomless shadow as he discards his pants. "I'm dying to be inside you, Fire Girl. You game?"

"Yes!" I want it bad enough to set the world ablaze.

Heat swells in my chest and ears, and I bite his neck, hard enough for it to leave a mark. He squeezes my ass and lifts me up.

Despite the proof of his riches, the grandeur of his bedroom, and the glow of his skin, when he's naked and hard for no one but me, I can almost believe we're the same.

"Enough!" Celeste Draco sneers from the doorway, and her deafening command echoes across the room.

Cole gently slides me off of him. He plucks his discarded jacket off the floor and wraps it around my frame. The hem falls above my knees, and I hold it closed.

Peaches and sin linger on my tongue.

Celeste points her gloved finger in my direction. "She is not welcome here."

Undisturbed by his nakedness, Cole places himself between us. "Julia Winslow is under my protection."

"We're at war, son." Celeste turns her attention to the head of the humongous bed. Her jewelled, midnight-blue skirt screeches against the marble as she glides closer to it. "We cannot waste our time on a mortal. Besides, we have no right to keep her. She's an earthling."

She grazes the books tucked in the headboard like she's perusing the stacks for a creepy bedtime story. "Osbourne has already written to me. He knew the witch would end up here. We negotiated an exchange." Her sugary tone chips away every last shred of dignity left in me.

"She freed Flynn. She's on our side," Cole growls.

Celeste tugs on the ends of her ballroom glove and rolls it off her arm. "Your silly infatuation is not important. Jessa is still stuck out there, and the mortal's presence in Faerie creates an opportunity to get her back. She needs our help. She needs *you*. Do I need to remind you how important her family is to our reign? How influential her father has become? Do what you will with your night, but the mortal leaves in the morning."

"No."

Celeste's monstrously cold eyes flash with power. "Colden Alaric Desirys, you will swear to do everything in your power to bring this girl to the throne room tomorrow at ten o'clock sharp, or I will take her *now*." Magic zaps in blue bolts over her one bare arm.

Cole cries out in pain, struck by an invisible fist. Tremors rock his body from head to toe before he offers his mother a stiff bow. "By the Dark Gods, I swear it," he grits through his teeth, his dark voice dripping with pain.

Celeste smiles. "Enjoy your night, mortal. You will never see the likes of Faerie—or my son—ever again."

An icy burst ripples through the air. Frost pinches my nose and dries up my throat in an instant. My teeth chatter at the sudden change in temperature, my entire body numb.

Celeste doesn't bother to close the door behind her.

Cole's lips turn blue, and his arms shake at his sides. Icicles frost over his lashes before he drapes an arm around me. "Breathe. Ride the wave out. Her magic can't take root inside you if you don't let it."

I force myself to breathe despite the ice, the despair. Finally, after a few long inhales and exhales, life returns to my limbs.

Cole presses his lips to mine softly. "That leaves us precious few hours to figure out how I'm going to break that promise."

15

DON'T FEAR THE REAPER

Jules

A mountain of books sprawls over the duvet when Flynn waltzes into the room. He stops cold at the sight of the mad librarian set-up. His powdery blue gaze travels from the borrowed undershirt I'm wearing to a half-naked Cole.

"I figured you guys would be done with the reunion sex by now, but these aren't post-coital faces." He points to each of us in turn. "What did I miss?"

"My mother." Cole dumps another book on the pile. He's searching his library for a way to thwart Celeste's plans.

I play with the hem of the oversized shirt. If only I was wearing underpants for this conversation. "Could Flynn smuggle me out of the palace?"

Cole shakes his head. "Ha! My mother probably posted guards at every door and turret." He throws a glance in my direction. "Even if you could, would you want to spend the rest of your life as a fugitive in Faerie?"

My throat tightens. Probably not. "I can't just greet Oz tomorrow morning and say, 'Hey, how you doin' buddy? Want to take me home and forget that I stole from you?'"

Flynn paces the room. "If Oz collects you in the morning... We all know what happens after that. It was stupid of us to come here. It's the perfect opportunity to get rid of you. A silly mortal girl runs away to Faerie and dies—it's too cliché."

The gruff, uncensored comment rubs me the wrong way. "My insignificance is noted."

Cole flips through the pages of a thick, leather-bound encyclopedia. "Flynn's got a point. You won't make it home, and he'll blame it on me."

I cross my arms. Adrenaline and fear run through my blood. "Are you saying there's nothing to be done? I can kick Oz's ass if needed." My jaw clenches. I might have squished the peeling hag, but I should probably not hurl infernal magic at Oz's head to see if it remains attached to his body. Killing Dark Falls' headmaster with forbidden magic means exile, and I'm no murderer. "There must be a way to resolve this without *too* much violence."

"If we trick him into staying in Faerie for a few days, we could enchant him," Flynn says.

Cole scoffs. "Oz will not be so naive as to hang out in Faerie. At best, he might be willing to make a deal. If he swears not to harm her, we could give the horn back—"

"No! He will not get Beth's soul. We have to free whatever magic is attached to it so that she can rest," I say quickly.

Cole cocks a brow. "Beth's soul?"

Flynn crawls over the book pile and lies down on the bed. Arms braced behind his neck, he stares at the ceiling. "You missed an episode. Beth's soul is still in the horn."

What if all this was for nothing? "Even if Oz promises to take me home in one piece, he'll be all too keen to enslave me with angel dust, so he can fuck me *and* my sister." I comb my hair back, dragging my fingers along my scalp like it'll somehow revive my dead brain. "I'm not giving the horn back to him. There must be something you can do."

"I need time. I can't *think*." Cole slams the last volume from the shelves on top of the others.

"You're a prince, are you not?" I don't know why I'm pushing his buttons so much. Panic has set root inside me.

"You don't belong here," he answers.

I push his chest, and the glare I serve him is half-angry, half-discouraged. We haven't found one tiny lead yet, and time is slowly ticking away.

"You know what I mean. You're not a citizen of Faerie, so there's nothing—" He freezes and turns to Flynn.

"What are you thinking?" I ask.

The earlier current of desperation and rage morphs into a restless, elusive energy as he turns back to me, clasping my upper arms. "Bear with me for a moment before you say no."

He stares deep into my eyes. "Marry me."

"Oh, for Queen Mab's sake!" Flynn rolls to his stomach, his face hidden in the pillow. "Dark mother, wake me from this nightmare," he adds, the words muffled.

A hiccup chokes me. "Whaa—Have you lost your mind?"

I wait for the punchline, but Cole looks dead serious. A little eager, even.

"It's the only way Oz doesn't leave with you tomorrow," he breathes.

"I don't want to marry you, Cole," I blurt out in a daze.

A dark shroud obscures his features, and I realize I need to fix my insensitive, knee-jerk answer. Him and his damn ego. He thinks it's about him.

"I don't want to marry *anyone*. I'm eighteen years old." I bite the insides of my cheeks.

The lines on his forehead ease. "Fae marriage is not at all what you're used to. It's not restrictive. It doesn't preclude us from marrying someone else."

My lips quirk at the insanity of this conversation. "Is that what you say to all the girls?"

He presses his fingers to the space between his brows. "Only the ones who do not wish to marry me. Which means just you, basically."

I stick out my tongue.

A deep inhale rocks his chest. "Jules. Oz can't afford for you to testify against him. He will kill you or enchant you or worse. Let me do this. Let me save your life and the horn. This way, we can regroup and find a better plan." His amber gaze pulses.

Doubts crumble in my mouth. There's no way I can marry Cole. No way.

He inches closer, his voice soft and non-threatening. "It's nothing more than a technicality. Plenty of people marry for citizenship. We wouldn't be the first."

The more he tries to frame this as a rational, bureaucratic move, the more my stupid heart entertains the idea. "Tell me all about it. In detail. What are the drawbacks? There must be *tons*."

"You will attract some unwanted attention from Fae purists who don't believe in cross-realm marriage."

"That's...weird but whatever." Cross-realm marriage. I didn't know that was even a thing.

"If you ever wanted to run for a political seat on the High Council, it will destroy your chances."

A dark chuckle escapes me. "My *other* problem prevents me from going into politics anyways. And I won't get elected for anything if I'm dead, so continue."

Demons can't run for office, can they? Maybe I'm being sarcastic. Maybe I'm being naive, but Gods, I don't find any of these drawbacks important. People already think I'm a Fae groupie. No one takes me seriously, and my future at Dark Falls is bleak considering I want to expose the headmaster for the fucker that he is. Even my ambition to become a Magus means nothing if the Magisterium is under the leadership of a two-faced murderer.

Cole squares his shoulders. "Servants will address you as your Highness."

"That's annoying, but doable. What else?"

He caresses the edge of my jaw with his thumb. "We would share a bond that can never be broken. Marriage is not just a promise here, it's an actual spell. I don't exactly know what that would mean for a mortal because it's never been done, but mated Fae and supernaturals sometimes share powers...and dreams."

A furious, rapid rhythm beats in my chest. This *technicality* is starting to sound like a fairytale. My forever might not last as long as his, but it'll be *something*. You can't forget your first wife, can you?

He laces and unlaces our hands like he can't quite stand still.

"If it's so harmless, why are you so eager?" I ask.

Energy ripples off him in waves. "What are you so afraid of?"

"Maybe you just want to own me."

His jaw ticks. "Maybe you just want to be remembered."

The statement tugs and twists at a deep, private wound inside my chest. The hidden desire rings true and vain and ugly, like a mortal's claim on eternity. Futile, and yet irresistible.

I do want to be remembered. If I do this, I'll be the first mortal to marry a Fae, the first earthling let into Seelie royalty.

A legend or a fool, but worthy of history either way.

That's almost enough to justify this folly, but not quite. I free my hands, about to refuse, when Cole's forehead touches mine.

Lids fluttering shut, he squeezes the nape of my neck with such care that I shudder. His chest heaves like the oxygen has been sucked from the room. "I'm a Fae prince. I'm expected to mess around until I'm fifty, then properly court a high-ranking Fae woman—or several —for a decade or two until I'm ready to start a family. With you, everything is different. I'll never have enough *time*. I've fallen hard and fast for you, against my better judgement and—let's face it—my survival instinct. You *burn* me, Jules Winslow."

The first woman Cole ever loved...

"I do want to be remembered. Most of all by you," I admit.

"And I need the whole world to know you're mine," he breathes.

The darkest, blackest parts of our souls are exposed. A desperate haste in his kisses loosens the spikes of uncertainty embedded in my heart. This is insane.

Impossible.

"Okay," I whisper.

A shaky breath passes through his parted lips. "Okay?"

"Yeah." The strangled acknowledgement spirals in my veins.

"By the Dark Gods and all their damned children, you guys are serious!" Flynn shouts from the pillow. His fist clenches around the edge of the duvet like it's somehow responsible for what just happened. "Fucking hell."

16

THE ASTUTE REDHEAD

Allie

*J*eremy's pale, shivering body lies on the infirmary bed. The private room, which housed Olson for many weeks, seems too small for the wolf's stature. The door creaks shut behind me, and Lydia Hawks twitches in her seat next to the werewolf, her small hand laced in his.

"How is he?" I ask quietly.

Her red-rimmed eyes betray her current state of mind, but she appears calm and collected when she says, "The same. The fever won't relent."

"What's the diagnosis?"

"They won't tell me a thing," she spits.

The venom in her voice surprises me—I didn't think those two were still dating.

Daniel ignored my messages, busy with the Magisterium and my mother, but I need answers. I've heard enough from their hushed conversations to know that Jules stole the horn. The fire was a diversion, and Lydia and Jeremy must have helped her. Jules had been spending so much time at Jeremy's recently; it only makes sense. If I can piece together where she went and find her before her involvement becomes public knowledge, before it's too late, I might be able to help her.

Sweat rolls down Jeremy's face, and he whimpers.

My heart hammers at the unnatural, desperate cry, and I grip his free hand.

"This is your fault," I tell Lydia, hoping to coax an emotional reaction out of her.

A stiff angle in her neck is all I get in response.

"If Jules hadn't stolen the horn, if you hadn't helped her, Jeremy would be fine." I speak the words as though I know them to be true.

Her jaw clenches, but she doesn't look at me, her gaze still locked on Jeremy. "Don't put this on me. You *killed* Elsbeth Eillis."

Eyes wide, I take a small step back. I expected this sort of comment from my sister, but her redheaded friend always appeared to be out of the loop, and a bit naive at best. "I was under a spell."

Lydia scratches the constellation of freckles on her neck. "Were you under a spell when you brushed us off for months? Or ignored Jules' questions? All this time, you were under a spell?"

Our eyes finally meet. Lydia stares right through me as though she read my destiny in her damn tarot cards and watched me drug Cole in her crystal ball.

My pulse drums a harsh rhythm in my chest. "Where is she?"

A wry smile tugs at the corner of her mouth. "Beyond your mother's slimy reach, that's for sure."

Out of mother's reach…

I grab her wrist and squeeze. "You helped Jules steal the horn and flee to Faerie? Are you completely insane? What if she gets eaten or killed? Or worse, what if she gets enslaved by a Fae? Have you thought about that at all?"

She shakes me off. "Okay, Blondie. Play the victim, like you always do. You've ignored your sister's existence from the day she arrived at the Academy. Don't pretend to care about her now."

"Fae are dangerous."

"*You* are dangerous. She's safer in Faerie than she ever was with you around."

My jaw clenches at the disgust in her tone, and I draw in a tight breath. Jules is in Faerie. I need to process. "Hate me all you want, but you disclosed her location. That was pretty dumb of you, if you ask me."

Lydia opens and closes her mouth, probably realizing her mistake, and flips me off.

I hustle out. Still, I got what I came for. I found Jules. Who cares if Lydia hates me? But tears threaten to pour over my eyelids, and the simple thought of Jules being alone in Faerie churns in my stomach.

I trek back to my room. The origami sculptures suspended above my head convulse at the force of my emotions.

A dragon. A unicorn. A phoenix.

What the fuck has my sister done? If the Seelie keep the horn, or if mother's illness progresses in the meantime, everything I've endured to get here, all the heartache, the regrets...it will all have been for nothing.

17

MADNESS

Jules

ole insisted that I meet with his head housekeeper, Mary, a Fae with clever eyes and a permanent sneer.

"I'm sworn to him. I could never betray his trust, no matter how much I want to." She walks in circles around me, one finger pressed into her chin dimple.

I haven't met a lot of female Fae, yet her glamor pales in comparison to the others. It's subdued, her skin a smooth shade of gray, and I wonder if it's a genetic trait, or a choice.

"You do not belong with him. You're a mortal." A long, defeated sigh punctuates the sentence. "But you'll die soon enough," she adds as though this marriage is palatable only in the sense that it won't last very long—to her anyway.

I flash my teeth. "If you don't want to do this, I don't need to wear a wedding dress."

"Tss—I will not let my Cole marry an ugly bride."

The Fae seamstress weaves her arms in front of herself and murmurs an incantation. Streaks of black-and-blue magic spark off her fingers. "Let your fire burn a little, so I can use it."

Flames lick my ribs, the release effortless in the face of the anxiety that's threatening to floor me.

Liquid silk bubbles into the air and glides across my skin. It feels fresh—but not cold—and weighs nothing. Black strips of cloth snake around my neck and leave my back and shoulders bare. Another wave rises from the seamstress' hands, and a flowy skirt with a glamorous side slit flows down my thighs. Speckles of red and orange wisp in and out of view along the lengthy skirt, and the fabric flickers a little more with each movement.

"A dress sewn in night and fire. A potent, irresistible, but destructive union. I hope you shine bright before you burn to ashes, mortal."

I raise a hand to the neck bow holding the dress in place and swallow hard. A demented Cinderella with her cruel, pessimistic Faerie godmother.

There's still time to stop the wedding. This is ludicrous. Worst idea ever.

And yet, as I catch a glance of my reflection in the round, freestanding mirror, I love what I see.

A Fae princess.

Greed burns at the back of my throat.

Am I doing this for power? Who am I trying to impress? Dad would freak out, Allie would be appalled and Lydia…

An elusive smile tugs at the corners of my mouth. Given the chance, Lydia would totally be my maid of dishonor.

Mary nudges my side. "What do you want me to do with your hair?"

Black, purple, and red curls tumble around my face in smooth, glossy waves, and I grin. "Leave it."

I will never be Fae, I have no magic glamor, but the hair is all me. It's unique and wild and slightly crazy.

I squeeze my mother's emerald pendant and shake out my shoulders. "I'm ready."

The scent of overturned earth hangs thick in the labyrinth of tunnels that runs under the palace. The crackles of the torch lights soothe my fears of being swallowed by shadows, each corner luring me deeper inside the maze.

Mary guides me forward. Accessible through ornate passageways, the palace's ceremonial hall is located below an immense Fae tree. Mary calls it the Hawthorn, a place of worship for their people.

The boys wait for me at the heart of the chapel.

Exposed rocks stick out of the walls of the interior chamber, and thick roots hang in beautiful swirly patterns above my head. Colorful lanterns hang from the nature-made chandelier.

One look at Cole stops my brain hamster cold in its tracks. The Fae prince I love is offering me the only immortality I can ever know, and I'm going to take it. Consequences be damned.

"That's a dress fit for a queen," Cole says, devouring me with his eyes.

Heat pools in my chest.

Mary clears her throat loudly and motions Cole aside. Despite her hushed tone, her disappointment is palpable.

I glide toward Flynn.

An elegant red jacket wraps around his shoulders, his hands linked at his front. The color highlights the tan he got over the last two days, his golden-white hair slicked back.

"If someone had said to me you would be the one to officiate my wedding…" I crack, trying to lighten the mood.

A raspy chuckle falls off his lips. "You and me both, Jules."

I stand stock-still in front of him. "Did you just call me Jules?"

"It's your name. You've said so about a thousand times."

"You never listened." Cole and Flynn refused to call me by my name for *months*, but the blond Fae was even more stubborn than his prince in that annoying habit.

He shrugs. "I wanted you gone. Now, it's never going to happen."

"Are you jealous?"

He roams my body up and down, his gaze lingering on the beauty mark on my shoulder. "Very."

I meant to tease Flynn for his obsession with Cole, but the response is everything but light.

The obsidian stone that serves as an altar shines in the dark. A perfectly circular pool of water—about a foot wide—flows around it. Despite the absence of a proper stream, the liquid swirls languidly around the altar like it's being stirred by an invisible hand.

Fresh moss and wildflowers bloom in thick patches in the lowest grooves of the stone—the tip of a black, shadowy iceberg. The unearthed rock clearly runs deeper into the earth than I could dream of. I ache to touch it, but the heady magical signature emanating from it gives me pause.

Cole returns to my side and captures my hand in his. "Are you sure about this?"

"Yes." The word trembles, but not the intent behind it. For whatever foolhardy, impossible reason, I want this, and not just to be remembered. If it's a dumb mistake, then so be it. I will go down in history as the dumb mortal who accidentally became a Fae princess. I can live with that.

Flynn rolls his eyes. "Let's do this thing before *I* change *my* mind."

Full-bodied shudders trickle down my spine, making my dress shine with bright embers. "What do I say?"

Cole squeezes my hand. "Whatever you want."

"What, no weirdly-phrased deals or back-handed promises? I don't have to swear my devotion to you or something?"

Cole cracks a smile. "We leave the deals to everyday life. Fae marriage is about trust, not obligation."

I can get behind that. I pat down the skirt of my fairytale dress with my free hand, unsure what to say. "Maybe we skip the vows?"

Cole's mouth curls down, but he quickly forces a neutral expression on his face.

I tug on his fingers. "I wish I could be eloquent and transparent about my feelings for you, in this crazy, beautiful moment, but I can barely think."

His shoulders relax, and he smiles, inching closer.

Flynn soaks his hand in the translucent pool at the foot of the altar. Clear droplets crawl up his hands, and his skin blisters at the contact. Tiny drops of water scatter over his arms like legions of tiny piranhas.

His forehead creases in a wince. "Uste garth."

I steal a glimpse at Cole.

"It means: I stand witness." The prince licks his bottom lip, his eyes glued to his friend.

Flynn coaxes out one end of a long, seemingly unending black ribbon—or is it a piece of algae?—from the restless current.

The dark thread sticks to my skin as Flynn wraps it across my wrist, then Cole's. Silver flecks glitter on the strange leaf. Light as smoke and deep as the night sky, it waves and weaves through the space between us, both solid and liquid at the same time.

Water climbs from the pool along the serpentine plant. My skin vibrates at its caress.

Flynn grips our wrists. The rough pads of his hands are chafed and red, as though a layer of skin has simply been peeled off, and his nails dig into my pulse point. "Elstebarst ste roan. Elstebarst ste ugne."

A ragged breath escapes Cole. "What was, is past. What is, always will be—it's a rough translation, but it essentially means forever."

Forever. For us, it means two different things.

The algae sinks into my skin, its sting feverish. I wince at the pain, but the sneaky eel-ribbon hisses happily as soon as it draws blood. It buries into my skin in a discrete, swirly tattoo. The rest of the thread, the part that was still connected to the water, worms its way back underneath the surface.

A shiver rattles Flynn's body, and he looks away for a mere moment before adding, "Elste u'run tan unillan."

Cole inches closer. "What you are and what I am are now one."

"Blood and soul. The melding has begun." Flynn frees us from his steel grasp.

I rub the fresh ink swirl.

Flynn drags his feet toward the entrance of the chapel. "I'll see you tomorrow."

"It's done?" I ask, surprised that the ritual would end so abruptly.

With one last, long look, he adds, "No, but you'll be happy that I didn't stick around until the end." A deep part of me feels his jealousy, his envy. It trickles down my skin like poisonous wine.

Cole caresses the bare plane of my lower back.

My ribcage expands painfully, tight and warm. "This is nothing like the weddings I'm used to."

He presses me to him. "Welcome to Faerie. Most weddings involve a lot of consummation, and a healthy dose of voyeurism."

"Let's concentrate on the first part." I glimpse at the ceiling of the earthy chapel.

He grabs my chin between his index and thumb and forces me to meet his gaze. "Don't be so nervous. We've done this before."

"Only once."

A wicked grin stretches his full lips. "Only one night." Cole pulls on one end of the bow behind my neck. The Faerie dress tumbles along my legs and hits the ground with a *swish*. I'm wearing nothing underneath. Mary assured me it was customary, but Cole's eyes widen.

He picks me up, and I wrap my thighs tightly around him as he walks right into the clear pool of liquid, the magic water not hurting him as it did Flynn.

He deposits me on the obsidian altar like fine jewelry on a velvet pillow. A jewel he wants to fuck.

"You're mine, at last," Cole groans, soft and yet totalitarian—a general who won the only war that was ever worth fighting.

"You do not own me," I repeat, but my voice is soft and teasing.

Cole presses his nose to mine. "But you own me. You've owned me since that day in the library, when you let me read the curse written across your back."

I'm shattered to learn this. "Then why were you such a jackass?"

His lips quirk. "I'm a Fae prince."

"For you, that explains everything away, doesn't it?"

"Always."

His bright smile melts my heart, and I don't care about the semantics anymore. Arms still linked behind his neck, I dive in for a kiss.

The altar is not quite wide enough for me to lie down. Its uneven shape offers a bit of support to my lower back, and it's at the exact right height for my thighs to rest comfortably around Cole's midriff.

With one hand, he unbuttons his medieval jacket.

Whispers chime along the stony walls, and the lanterns flicker. The rock below my ass pulses to life.

I cower closer to Cole. He warned me that the spell might get a little weird. Unwanted, incorporeal guests apparently crash all royal Fae weddings.

Magic presses on my shoulders, and the tremble in my bones alerts me to the presence of a dark, powerful energy.

"I got you, Fire Girl. Don't be afraid." A small area next to his collarbone blurs. Finger-shaped grooves ply his skin—almost like a helping hand. The jacket—and pants—dissolve into smoke.

Unintelligible voices stir the air next to my ear, but my eyes find nothing but shadows. *A healthy dose of voyeurism*…the statement wasn't restricted to Flynn.

Ghosts—spirits—whatever they are…we're not alone.

"They are harmless," Cole adds as though he read my thoughts.

Sinister snickers echo through the chapel. Our incorporeal hosts disagree, and I sink my nails into Cole's neck, unsure I can follow through.

He grazes the hot flesh between my thighs. The slickness he finds there drives me wild, and he gives a snarl that's more beast than man. Flames dance below the skin of my hips and thighs, my core throbbing harder with each breath.

I feel lightheaded and exposed, but Cole's kiss tethers me to this moment. My body doesn't mind our phantasm audience, and the more I think about them watching us, the more aroused I become. It's kinky and wild, but I'm way more into it than I thought I'd be.

Wings flicker at Cole's back. Wisps of black and blue Fae magic ripple along the sinews of his arms. Red flecks burn in his savage amber stare, his full Fae form unleashed, reminding me of that day in the Duel ring when I knocked us both unconscious. Purple and orange sparks rise from my skin and join the fray.

Little bits of my soul seem to rise along with them.

I curse under my breath when he bites and licks my hard nipples, teasing them in turn, the ache impossible to soothe.

My brain goes blank, and my heart thuds harder than the magic spicing up the air. My dark prince never breaks eye contact as he buries his dripping cock all the way inside me, so deep my toes curl and my breath vanishes.

A hot pocket of air glides along my shoulders, and I draw in a sharp inhale. Cole builds to a slow grind, the rush so sweet and heady that I cry out. The stone below me presses on my ass—invisible wraith hands rise from the altar to hold me snug and steady, ripe for the picking.

The primeval ritual disjoints a burrowed piece inside me and tugs and twists at it until I'm panting. I feel...pulverized. Different.

This is dark Fae magic, to be sure. Nothing in my realm ever releases so much fury and bliss. So much sin. The link between our bodies, like everything else about my prince, is addictive and devious.

Even in marriage, he corrupts me.

Cole increases his rhythm. The snaps of his hips both give and steal from me, and I arch my back, nails embedded in his shoulder blades.

A pair of ghostly lips graze my shoulder.

I give in to the desire they incite in me, welcoming their touch.

Pleasure scratches at the seams of my body, threatening to tear me apart. Not an orgasm—but a slow, delicious death. The end of my old life.

The spirits' hands pinch the flesh of my ass and breasts, emboldened by my surrender. My mouth opens in shock, and my vision blurs. My walls pulse, over and over again, the endless abyss of lust created by the spell never stopping my fall.

Heated groans resonate through the ether. The ghosts rob fragments of my release, their intrusion meant to alleviate the emptiness of eternity. Their greedy, elusive touches leave me outside myself, basking in the remnants of previous weddings celebrated on this altar of wicked passion and everlasting commitment.

Cole barely holds in a scream as he fills me with his release. The ecstasy in the pinch of his lips and the strain of his abs clue me in that this is new to him, too. He's not in control.

We both need a minute—or two—for the aftermath of pleasure to soothe the fire. We catch our breaths, half-sprawled over the obsidian stone, my elbows propped up behind me and my legs dangling from the edge. Cole holds part of his weight with his arms to spare me.

The spirits retreat to the shadows, sated by our performance. I can almost hear their satisfied commentary rustling down the earthy confines of the chapel.

I bring a shaky hand to my brow. "That was…something else," I croak, somehow already missing the fullness of Cole inside me.

I wiggle to stand, but he kisses me hard.

He pins me in place with his hip. "Don't you dare. I finally have you all to myself."

I do not care for words anymore, and neither does he. I need more. We're breaking all the rules doing this. Writing history. The spell might be over, but my hunger for him, his body, and his world, has only just begun.

18

CANNOT BE UNDONE

Jules

$\mathcal{I}$ stir awake at the sound of sheets ruffling. My head pounds. A painfully delicious sting burns my abs and legs—and the space between my thighs. We forgot to close the blinds last night, and the early morning light hurts my eyes. Whispers skitter around the large bedroom, and I glimpse at the door where Cole—a very naked Cole—chats with Mary. Our gazes meet across the room. He returns quickly to my side and envelops me in a warm, dizzying embrace.

I rest my head on the fresh silk of the pillow. "Can we stay here?"

"I have a deal to honor," he grumbles behind my ear.

Right. He needs to take me to his mother. The thought ruins my lazy mood and sparks an icy flare along my neck.

Cole places a small golden box on the pillow.

I shuffle to my knees on the bed, holding the sheet to my chest.

He looks at me expectantly. "Open it."

My fingers shake as I grab the box and hold it to the light. It's made of real gold. The box itself must be worth a fortune in the mortal world.

"It's not a ring," Cole adds quietly. I detect a hint of worry in his hushed tone.

The box clicks open, and all the spit dries from my mouth. A single ear cuff dazzles under the sun beams with copper, silver, and brass accents. The pure, intricate metal threads form an artsy, feminine piece of jewelry.

I pinch the shell of my ear. "You don't like my round ears?"

He inches closer, his chuckle soft on my cheek. "I *love* your round ears."

I can hardly breathe. "It's beautiful."

"*You* are beautiful."

I almost scoff at the ridiculousness of being called beautiful by a Fae prince, but somehow, I can't. This isn't the time or place to dwell on my insecurities, but it does drill some much needed sense into me.

"Do you have your Academy gear close? Cauldrons, ingredients?" There's a little—huge—detail I forgot to deal with last night.

He rests his chin on my shoulder. "Why?"

"I need to make a contraceptive potion." My cheeks heat up, but hell, it's the truth. Somehow, all the sex we had last night—even the spirit kink—embarrasses me less than talking about contraception. What a poor testimonial for my mainstream mortal upbringing.

Cole's face wrinkles in the most genuine, adorable way. "You don't need to take anything. It's not an issue. Fae can choose to be fertile or not."

I turn to face him. "Are you for real?"

"It's not like: oh, tonight, I'll be fertile, but not tomorrow. It takes weeks for biology to work its magic, but we do have some power over the process. I'm definitely not ready for children."

"That's so...practical." I'm not sure I'm comfortable leaving that responsibility to him and him alone, but I trust his answer. "Do you have any other super powers? Can you regrow a limb if severed? Can you see through stone?" I joke, trying to mask the tinge of humiliation in my voice. Clearly, I don't know the first thing about Fae biology.

He winks. "Not yet."

My intolerable heart swoons, and he draws me in for yet another kiss.

I never thought of myself as a romantic person. I scoffed during Hollywood movies and rolled my eyes at the incessant loving whispers my high school peers exchanged during lunch time.

Being in love feels raw and uncertain, and I don't quite understand why I agreed to marry Cole, or why he asked in the first place. He's not human.

In the face of dawn, is Fae citizenship an excuse to justify this folly? What if our attraction for one another simply grew into a monster neither of us could control?

I'm scared that Cole will regret marrying me. We talked at length about what I was giving up, but he didn't once mention what the drawbacks were *for him*. Big oversight on my part.

Mary laid out a few dresses for me to choose from, but I select a black and white ensemble of simple pants and a tunic, instead. Golden threads highlight the cuffs and collar with letters in the Fae alphabet. I wouldn't know where to start with most of the more traditional women's gowns, anyway.

Faerie clothes aren't restricted to mystical, magically sewn midnight dresses. The fast fashion garments I'm used to, and the expensive Academy uniforms, don't hold a candle to the fabrics in this realm. The puff sleeves of the white tunic run past my wrists, and the lace-up pants are easy to adjust and comfortable.

Cole and I can barely keep our hands off each other as we get dressed.

Once we're semi-decent, he clasps my hand in his and leads me through the maze of corridors. The link between our fingers electrifies me. I wonder if cherry wood would numb the thrill in my bones, or if a cup of salt might tame me back to reason.

I suspect all the salt in the three realms wouldn't make a lick of difference.

The throne room comes into view, and Cole stiffens. He places a soft kiss on my wrist, in the exact spot where the wedding ritual left its mark, before he ushers me along. I roll my shoulders back and follow him into the space that almost unraveled me yesterday. A place where I felt like nothing but a flea begging for a prince's crumbs of affection.

It's surreal, and my blood races.

Celeste Draco wears a sleeveless dress that hugs her upper body before it swirls around her hips and waves to the floor in a glittering, silver-and-blue train.

"You're early." She sounds pleased until her eyes fall upon me. I'm not sure exactly what she sees, but immediately, her eyes darken. Her entire body—from the tip of her bare toes to the sparkling diamonds on her tiara—goes rigid.

She knows, and while I'm not sure how, the clench of her jaw makes me practically giddy.

A distorted chuckle passes her lips. "Your father will beat you bloody." The empty sound brings a chill to my neck.

Cole spares a long look to our joined hands, and a secretive, joyful smile ghosts over his lips. "As true as that may be, she is mine now. It cannot be undone."

The guards behind the lounge chairs remain stoic, but whispers buzz across the handful of courtiers present, and quite a few stolen glances glide along my shoulders.

Under the watchful eyes of her subjects, Celeste swallows back her ice magic. She shakes her head and smiles like Cole is nothing but a toddler. "I will not waste any more time on this. You can show our guests out when they arrive."

The power dynamics are shifted here, and I realize that, while she might be a Fae queen, Cole actually outranks her in the eyes of the court.

Cole releases me and sits on the chaise-longue, his back hunched forward. His sight latches on to the main entrance. "It'll be my pleasure to send that dragon back where he belongs."

Celeste whistles out the back, and the guards on either side ease up slightly after she's gone.

I take the chair where Cole's sister, Helena, sat the day before and force myself not to fidget. The velvet cushions invite you to lean back and relax. It's a strange throne room. It doesn't look quite as intimidating as the ones in movies. Instead of: *look how powerful and deadly I am*, it says: *how dare you interrupt my nap?* I guess the Seelie court doesn't need skulls or knives to assert their reign.

They rule with temptation.

A nasty voice in my head chants. *You don't belong here. You don't belong here.*

In a flash, I'm back to feeling like the outsider that I am, stuck in a place where I don't know the rules. A realm I was told scary stories about ever since I was a child. A world where mortals live and die for their rulers.

I grip the armrests.

What the fuck have I done?

The sprite guard by the entrance flaps his wings before Oz comes into view. The smug look on his face slaps me back to reality.

Two Magisterium agents trail behind him, escorting Jessa. The Fae has her blue hair braided in a crown on top of her head. Her cruel stare travels from Oz to Cole, avoiding me thoroughly.

"Where is the Queen?" Oz asks.

"She had other dragons to fry."

Oz's gray stare collides with mine. "You stole from me, Julia."

The amicable demeanor infuriates me. I open my mouth to tell him to go to hell, but Cole beats me to it. "She only took back what you stole from me. Isn't that the story you're going with?"

"Wow, the cruel prince is in love. Who would have thought that, after all the girls you *plowed* through, this one would hold your attention for more than a minute." Oz rubs his brow, his lips pursed like this is all a bad joke. "You still have to give her to me."

Cole stands abruptly, but he rectifies his speed and strolls to the top of the steps with the same devil-may-care apathy he demonstrated when I arrived at court. "Get out, Osbourne. You're not welcome on my lands." The nonchalant command echoes throughout the halls.

Goosebumps run up my arms.

In the human realm, Oz is the best sorcerer, but here… Here, Cole reigns.

The dragon shows his teeth. "The Council gave me an order. You can't keep a citizen of the realm in Faerie against our wishes."

Magic pulses from his open palm and reverberates across my skin. Magisterium agents used that type of magic on me when I got arrested, but the immense pull I felt then is barely an itch now.

Cole angles his chin in my direction, and his eyes pulse with a tinge of affection—and a shitload of cupidity. "She's no longer a citizen of the realm. She's mine."

Oz's arm falls at his side. "You fool, this goes way higher than me."

Jessa's eyes are wide with more than surprise. She searches the room for something, and a shiver shakes her graceful body from head to toe.

Cole raises a hand in her direction. "Jessa stays, of course."

Oz curls and uncurls his fist and gives Jessa, his hostage, a quick glance. "This wasn't the deal."

"You can't keep a citizen of Faerie from me against her wishes." Cole smiles with more teeth than warmth. "Jessa, do you wish to stay?"

Jessa gives him a quick nod.

Oz's arms blur as though he's about to shift and fly out the glass ceiling, but he turns to me instead. "Have you lost your mind?"

I tilt my head to the side. "Jealous? Are you the only man allowed to find me *fascinating*?"

The venom-coated words bring me back to that night in his cabin where he kissed me. I beat him at his own game. I used him while he thought he was using me, and I stole the horn. I've escaped his grasp now, and I will find a way to wrench Allic out of his toxic influence if that's the last thing I do.

Oz gauges me for a minute, his gray eyes dark and dangerous. "Have you figured out his true motives, yet?"

I bite my tongue, knowing I shouldn't dignify his efforts to turn me against Cole with a response.

"Oh, Miss Winslow…you're even dumber than your sister." The

confidence written in the snide curve of his lips erodes mine. "Power-ful, but dumb...doomed to repeat the same mistakes as their father."

What the fuck is he talking about? What mistakes? I school my features into an unwavering mask, but fire swells in my gut. What secrets does Oz hold over my family? I don't trust him one bit, but Cole's ashen face tells me the dragon struck a cord.

Once again, the sting of magic prickles my skin.

What if Cole didn't tell me the whole truth?

19

INDECENT PROPOSAL

Jules

Golden tapestries blur at the edge of my vision, and the palace's walls close in on me as I bolt out of the throne room. Vertical stripes in the stained glass windows scintillate under the red Fae sun, royal prison bars meant to mesmerize the weak. The opulence of the decor suffocates me.

I wish I could remember the quickest way to a balcony, because I'm simply gasping for air.

"Jules!" Cole shouts, but I ignore him.

Fire magic writhes beneath my palms, begging to be set loose.

He chases after me. "Jules, stop!"

This time, his plea jolts me back to reality. The acrid scent of burnt clothes stings my nose, my control over the magic slipping. Cinders pepper the tunic I'm wearing, and the blaze will soon scorch my skin.

I spin around. "What was Oz talking about?"

Cole's bare feet squeak against the checkered hallway as he comes to an abrupt stop. "Oz babbles."

"No. Answer me." I dig my fingers into his lower arm.

"Infernal magic."

"Short answers won't cut it. Elaborate, *your Highness*," I clip.

He moves to tuck a curl behind my ear, but I slide back a few feet, daring him to try again. If he thinks he can sweet talk me into submission, he's got a fireball coming for his face.

His hand hangs awkwardly in the air before he scratches the back of his neck. "Oz implied that I married you for your powers. He wanted to drive a wedge between us."

"Half an hour ago, I felt fine—perfect even—but now…" I bring a hand to my chest, my breathing still ragged. Fire builds below my emerald pendant, oblivious to my commands. "That throne room is enchanted or cursed—or enchanted to feel like a curse."

Every time I step within these gold-plated walls, I feel small and insignificant. My nerves hammer at my insecurities as delicately as a troll with a stone club.

Cole averts his gaze. "Yes. It's Fae magic at its finest. An insidious spell that escalates negative emotions and anxieties about ones-self. Even I am not totally immune."

The ache in my ribs eases. My witchy-instincts were right, and I'm not entirely to blame for the treacherous doubts that invaded my mind.

"Funny how you forgot to mention it yesterday," I growl.

"We never got around to it."

I huff and escape to a nearby interior courtyard, the fire still raging inside me.

A fountain spurts translucent water out into the air, and the breeze blows a soothing mist on my face. A mermaid statue with her breasts bare and a crown of rainbow fishes at her brow stalks us quietly. We're nowhere close to Cole's quarters, and the seaweed and foam colors of this wing remind me of Brie's scales.

I pause. "Where are we?"

"In the Sea Queen apartments." He forges ahead of me. "Don't listen to Oz. His Faerie portal spit you out near Unseelie territory. He must know how precarious our borders truly are and how important a power like yours could become in the war against them."

He stands next to the fountain and plays with one of the water jets.

I watch his face. The dark glint in his eyes quickens my pulse, but I read nothing but truth in them, and my suspicions waiver. The clammy hold of the throne room lessens, and fresh droplets extinguish my flames.

I drag my nails along the ridge of the inked scar the wedding ritual branded in my wrist. "Brie's mother lives here?"

"Sometimes."

I knew mermaids were inter-realms travellers, but I had no idea Brie's family was so close to Cole's. It explains how well Cole and Brie know each other, and why they probably fucked. Oz's *plowing* comment buzzes in my ears like an armor-plated bee, oblivious to my attempts to swat it off my mind.

Cole rubs my arms up and down. "We can't stay in the palace. My mother will make our lives miserable. We'll go to my place."

"Your place?"

He runs his wet fingers through his jet-black hair. "My estate."

I poke his upper arm. "Spoiled prince."

He nudges my side. "Paranoid mortal."

Instead of heading for his bedroom, Cole leads me to a cul-de-sac at the back of his personal wing. A copper and silver door at the end of the corridor absorbs all the light of the torches, this section as window-less as the servants' stairs.

Fae magic zaps along Cole's palms as he flatters them to the metal. The door whines on its hinges, and we tip-toe into a dark room.

I grow a ball of fire in my hand to see better. In the middle of the room, a Faerie portal reflects its orange and red hues. The six-foot tall mirror hangs from the ceiling, held by translucent cables reminiscent of spider-webs. Shadows undulate in the glass.

I raise my hand to the rainbow-streaked surface, surprised to see my reflection—and not some terrible Fae version of myself. "Darth-Jules is gone."

Cole's brows form a straight line. "Darth-Jules?"

"My Faerie alter-ego," I chime, testing the feel of the event horizon before we walk through it. My fingers disappear in its depths, but the portal doesn't suck me in. Technically, my hand is now stuck somewhere between worlds. Like my soul.

"You've assimilated a bit of my magic. Basic Fae glamors should not affect you any more, not at the rate they did before." Cole gently reels my hand back.

"Ow." I wince at the sudden, unexpected sting. Frost bites my flesh, and I bring my blue fingers to my mouth.

"Careful with that. It's not a toy."

"Too bad my newfound Fae magic can't swallow the effects of the throne room." I close my eyes, trying to sense the change in myself. In him. I haven't slept enough. I'm wary of this new world, but other than that, there's no "on" switch for whatever *upgrade* I inherited.

"I've got a bit of your magic, and you've got a bit of mine." I straighten the front of the Fae tunic. "Doesn't sound as dire as Oz implied."

Cole clears his throat, suddenly looking all serious. "To set the record straight—you're okay with the fact that I married you for your powers now that you have some of mine as well?"

His wide grin turns my brain to mush, but I slap his chest.

He spins me around to face the glass again, his hands massaging both my shoulders. "After you."

The specifics of Faerie travel elude me. Cole could *zap* from anywhere in Dark Falls to Faerie without a proper gate like this one, but he clearly can't teleport at will around Faerie.

I dig my heels into the marble to resist his light push. "How does it work, exactly? Can you build portals wherever you want? Why was Dark Falls different?"

A puff of air caresses my cheek. "I'll explain it in detail, but not today. Today, I'm taking you to my favorite place in the three realms. We haven't slept nearly enough, I'm famished, and you're grumpy as hell."

"I could *still* get grumpier."

"We'll go to my place for a day or two. Figure this all out. Let the dragon digest his failure. We need to come up with a real plan—one that doesn't end with either of us in a Magisterium cell—or worse."

I grip his hand and crane my neck to see him. "What about the horn?"

The confident look on his face soothes my fears. "I'll ask Mary to pack our things and send Flynn a note. They'll catch up with us later. We can't solve all of our problems—expose Osbourne, clear my name, fix Dark Falls, end the bigotry between our realms—in one day."

The offer is too tempting to resist. "Alright. I'll give you a few days. But then, we need to act."

FAERIE BREAD SIMPLY melts on your tongue. The pastry reminds me of a trip to Hawaii, with its purple shade and the sweet, fluffy butter. The late morning meal soothes my nerves and brings a semblance of normalcy to the whirlwind that has become my life since I left Dark Falls. With all the chaos, I simply had forgotten to eat.

Cole shows me around his *estate*.

Marble halls and golden doorways are nowhere to be found here, the atmosphere closer to a fancy—but very human—mountain lodge. Exposed wood beams run above our heads, and the windows open to the excited chatter of small, round, yellow birds with bright pink eyes.

Cole admires the one closest to us. "They're called *Melhei*, for their melodic chants."

Whenever he speaks his native tongue, I want to rip his clothes off.

A stone chimney divides the main living area in two, and I pick out a few history books from the shelves on each side of the fireplace, determined not to remain illiterate about this new realm and its inhabitants. When we circle back to the main room, Cole guides me past a row of retractable glass panes to a patio. A bright, pleasant morning replaces the stuffy Mellen humidity. Crooked rocks form a staircase that descends toward a waterfall. The medium-sized stream spills into an emerald basin, not quite as tall as the one in Dark Falls, but ten times more beautiful.

Cole gestures to the ground. "Watch your step, it can get slippery after a rainfall."

Puddles of rain squish below the balls of my feet as we head down to the water.

"You're always barefoot here," I note. "Why?"

"Wearing shoes disconnects us from the magic in the soil. Power runs deep below the surface of our lands. Mary can bring you a pair of flats if it bothers you."

"It's okay. I was just curious." Magic in the soil. If the obsidian rock from yesterday is any indication, Faerie's geological formations will be interesting to study. Beth's notes and speech about Dark Falls' center and the experiments done on it over the years to "mine" out its energy might even relate.

Up-close, the emerald basin stuns my senses. The surrounding mist holds a sweet scent of sunshine and vanilla. Orchid-shaped flowers snake along the rocks. Their aerial roots create beautiful patterns over the electric-blue moss. Pink, purple, and white petals sway in the breeze.

I inhale deeply.

A wood platform runs up to the edge of the water, a lounge chair and a small, white cabana installed where the trees are scarce and allow for the sun to pass through the intricate vegetation.

Cole shrugs off his jacket and pants and jumps into the pond. He's submerged to his shoulders, but the clear water magnifies the green rocks near his feet as though they are inches from my face.

"I don't have a bathing suit," I say with a smile, very aware that Cole doesn't give a damn.

He splashes me playfully. "You don't need one."

"Are we going to strategize, or have sex?"

Cole's face crumples. "Who says we can't do both—though preferably *not* at the same time."

With one last look around to make sure we're alone, I strip. Cole licks his lips like a panther waiting for its next meal.

Faerie water flows along my skin. It's lighter than I'm used to, and warmer than I expected. I dive under the surface and hum, the smoky taste of charcoal detectable on my tongue.

Cole chases me down the length of the basin and grabs me from behind in a bear hug. My heart somersaults. It's still so new, so foreign for us to touch so freely. I try to live every moment to the fullest, knowing this quite literal honeymoon phase will soon pass.

Reality awaits. I can't stay in Faerie forever, can I? I have a duty to Beth to expose her real killer, and I can't drop out of school. Allie needs me to knock some sense into her. Faerie time zones might not work in my favor much longer, and I can't afford to lose my head.

I kiss Cole hard to forget about the outside world for one more minute. He hauls me onto a flat rock on the opposite side of the platform. Droplets sprinkle my breasts, and Cole drinks them off my skin one by one. We kiss until we're breathless.

His nails streak along my ass, and I let out a ragged moan when Cole pins me down.

His slick, hot breath caresses my ear. "Flynn is at the top of the stairs."

Eyes wide, I stiffen in his arms. I can't see the top of the stairs from here—nor the windows of the lodge, but birds fly overhead, maybe disturbed by Flynn's arrival. The heavy rush of the stream drowns out all sound.

Cole holds my hands above my head to prevent me from fleeing. "He came to talk, I'm sure. But now that he knows what we're doing…" He punctuates his statement with a grin, slipping all the way inside me .

I bite my bottom lip to stifle a groan and wrap my legs around him.

"He's contemplating his options, probably wishing he could strike us both from his heart." Cole rests his forehead on mine, moving inside me so languidly it drives me half-mad.

The roof of my parched mouth itches with thirst. "Oh?"

Cole nibbles on my ear. "Don't pretend that you don't know. Flynn is smitten with you. I saw it as soon as you two arrived."

I swallow hard. "He loves *you*."

Cole switches both my wrists to one hand. "Yes, but he also envies me. He both wants to be *with me* and *be me*. It fucks with his brain." His free palm glides down the hollow of my neck to my belly button. "Did you like it? When you kissed him?"

A nervous stutter whizzes out of my lungs. "Err—Flynn annoys the fuck out of me."

Heat builds in my chest, my breasts so full and heavy that Cole's caresses turn to sweet, sweet torture. I could easily break free from his hold if I wanted, but I love the predatory look on his face.

Mischief and desire mingle on his breath. "That's not what I asked."

Isn't he angry that I kissed his friend? My ribs rise and fall. "Why are you saying it like it's a good thing?"

"Why are you so wet?" he chuckles darkly.

I can't deny how close I am to a blinding orgasm. My body craves all the kinks my mind was taught to avoid, and the fact that Flynn might actually be watching totally riles me up.

Cole teases me, one deep stroke at a time. "You asked me once if Flynn and I used to fuck. You've clearly thought about the possibility…"

My lids flutter. I've thought about it a million times. It drives me wild and liquifies my gut, but I can't bring myself to say it.

Cole stops, and my hips thrash in disappointment.

He twists my breasts with his large hand, each wicked pinch peeling away my embarrassment. "What happens in Faerie…"

"…stays in Faerie? Is that—" I groan as he switches sides again— "what Fae marriage is like?"

A heavy breath rushes past my collarbone. "Only if you want it to be."

By the Dark Gods! He's actually asking.

My gaze flies to Cole's tattoos, and despite the heat in my belly, I shake my head. "I told you before…one psycho at a time, thank you very much."

He laughs, his head tilted back, and the joyous sound trickles all over my fiery skin. His beauty shines so bright, I think I might faint. I purr as he picks up the pace. Despite the soreness, the tender flesh between my thighs is still ravenous for the feel of him.

His hold on my wrists hardens. "Then at least let him hear you scream."

20

ELISHEBA

Jules

Nestled in Cole's arm, I stir awake. A suffocating breeze creeps up my legs, and my skin tingles with the feverish bite of impending danger. My eyes snap open in time to see a blue-tinged spear descend upon me.

I jerk upward, but Cole's weight prevents me from moving.

The pointy end of the spear presses between my lover's shoulder blades. An armored Fae warrior maneuvers the pole. His yellow chainmail gleams in the sunlight.

"Philandering and murder. Is that really what I taught you, boy?" The salt-and-pepper hair of the massive Fae flies around his head, the thick strands obscuring the sky. Deep cracks stretch the corners of his clouded eyes. "You could never keep your head straight with a pretty girl present."

Cole turns to face our attacker, and his hands fly up in surrender.

A heavy shroud of magic presses on my shoulders, my arms, my face.

"Get off her." The Fae gestures for Cole to move to the side.

My prince rolls off me without a sound and crouches with his hands held up in a halting motion, the way you approach a roaring dragon.

The resemblance strikes me then. The masculine, angular cheekbones of the two men follow the same curve, and their proud noses are almost identical. A pout twists both their mouths with an air of snobbery and lassitude. The few words uttered by the stranger were enough to convince me that they know each other, but he's clearly family. Definitely not a random dude hunting for reckless newlyweds.

Sweat drips down my neck, and flames lick my chest at how exposed I am. The fire creates a painful shield between me and the man's stare. Scanning the intruder from head to toe, I search for the best way to disarm him. Family or not, he shouldn't threaten us with blunt weapons.

Infernal magic tickles the inside of my palms. "Who are you?"

"*Silence.*" The stranger nicks Cole's neck with the edge of the blade.

I open my mouth, and my tongue moves, but no sound comes out. Lips stuck in a perfect "o," I grab my throat. My arms and legs grow heavy, as if severed from the rest of my body—thankfully only metaphorically.

Gods! Does every rabid lunatic in Faerie possess his own Jules off-switch?

The man is Cole's relative, but not the King. I would know if the King of Faerie stood in front of me.

"Did you kill Elisheba Eillis?" The ancient name rolls off the warrior's tongue in a rich, multifaceted accent.

Beth... I guess she didn't always go by that name.

Cole holds his gaze. "Yes."

My jaw slacks, the adrenaline spikes in my blood, and my lips move faster and faster, trying to rectify the story, but I'm mute and helpless.

The Fae's lids flutter, his back hunched at Cole's answer. A short, painful sigh wheezes out of his tight mouth. "Why?"

Cole wraps his hand around the pole of the spear, right behind the sharp head, and sinks it a little deeper inside his skin. "Angel dust."

The shaft trembles in the old Fae's hand. "*Ennarrii ttou eschne.*"

"*Eschne meerth.*" His eyes are feral, almost daring his opponent to slice his head off—or better yet, calling his bluff.

With a grunt, the warrior staggers backward. The lethal obscurion finally retreats from my lover's neck.

He points to me and says, "*Fenet oust karinina?*"

Cole stands. "A witch."

The man rolls his eyes. "*Stogg!*"

I do not have to know ancient Fae to interpret the meaning of that last part. The dull, irksome pressure on my windpipe eases at last, and I spring to my feet. "Who are you?" I repeat.

A thick wool coat appears out of thin air at my feet. I slip it on and straighten the lapels to keep a smidge of composure.

The Fae motions for me to sit. "Down, little girl. I have no interest in you."

I fall to my ass on the rock. My pubic bone screams in pain. "Stop doing that!" Magic dances in my bones, and a strong undercurrent of infernal fire crackles beneath my skin. "Let me stand up, or by the Dark Gods—"

Sometimes, even *family* needs a punch of forbidden magic in the face.

A piercing amber gaze, so similar to Cole's, steals my thoughts. His age only enhances the other-worldly beauty, the beckoning Fae magic. The sorcerer tilts his head as purple flares spark off my skin.

Cole clears his throat, managing to remain princely despite his nakedness. "Why are you here, uncle?"

Uncle. There. Wasn't so difficult.

The magical hold releases my muscles as Cole's *uncle* walks away. "I came to kill you. Now, I'm partial to a drink. Get dressed, *lillem*. You have a lot to explain."

I tie the coat's sash over my stomach. I really need to keep my clothes on more.

Spear-yielding uncle buries the head of his scary pole in the grass and passes his chainmail over his head before he sits in the cabana, at the edge of a black velvet lounge chair that's part of a matching set.

A bucket of ice keeps a bottle of champagne cold in the narrow space between the chairs. Two half-full flutes glisten with condensation on the table in the corner.

The Fae digs a flask from his interior pocket, uncorks the top, and raises it in cheer. "To young fucking love."

"Cheers." I snatch a champagne flute and down it in one gulp. The citrus and bubbles return a bit of life to my body, my muscles still stiff from the man's invisible hold—and the sex-on-rocks situation.

Cole grabs a white towel from the table and washes the blood dripping from his neck. "When did you get here?"

"I came here as soon as I heard. Took you long enough to join, but I couldn't attack you at the palace, could I?"

Cole chucks out a dark laugh, and it confirms my hunch that his uncle was actually prepared to kill him.

We observe each other for a minute. Maybe two. The silence stretches and expands.

"Are Fae family meetings always so tense?" I joke. Knowing Cole, it shouldn't surprise me. Serves me right to forget what I married into.

"Erron, Jules. Jules, Erron," Cole says with a smirk, and I know him well enough by now to suspect Erron is somewhat of a friend—blood-shedding, murderous tendencies aside.

The flask runs out, and Erron shakes it upside down with a puzzled look as though he can't believe it's already empty. He drags the back of his tattooed hand across his lips. Fae alphabet decorates each of his knuckles.

"Who ground the angel dust?" His gruff tone remains steady, but his amber irises dim.

Fear drums in my veins. I'm sure that, if Cole's answers aren't satisfactory, the spear might come into play again.

Cole plays with his colorful rings. "Daniel Osbourne, Dark Falls' new headmaster."

"How did you do it?"

"She was unconscious when I got there. Ripe for the kill."

"Was he acting alone?" Erron's quick interrogation is meant to leave no time for fibs.

Cole nods. "As far as we know."

I swallow hard, grateful that Cole didn't mention Allie's existence.

Erron rubs his earrings between his index and thumb, and the twist of jade and amber rings a bell.

"You're Beth's old flame," I say.

His eyes snap to mine. "How would you know that?"

The tremble of power rolling off him begs me to inch back, but I dig my toes into the plush carpet of the cabana and hold my ground. "Her ring had the same color-scheme as your earrings."

"She wore my ring?" In that question, I see the first hint of weakness, the hunch of his spine deepening.

I chew on my bottom lip. I don't want to outright lie, but it seems cruel and unnecessary to set the record straight. Who knows, maybe she did wear his ring.

He changes the subject. "You're that half-demon baby girl."

"You were the one that bound my powers," I dead-pan, my mind piecing together Beth's confidences with the reality of this *Erron*, the Fae shaman she used to love.

Cole refills both our glasses, hanging on every word.

Erron and I measure each other with tilted chins and thin lips. He finally sees me as something more than a piece of ass.

"She broke the curse and freed your powers. Why?" he asks.

I rap my fingers against the champagne flute. "Why not?"

He leans back in his chair, his legs spread on each side. "Hmmpf."

"Are you a Desirys, or a Draco?" I ask.

Cole chokes on a mouthful of champagne.

"Don't insult me, witch," Erron hisses.

A Desirys, then. I play with the wide buttons of the trench coat, suddenly remembering that this man saw me in my birthday suit, his weirdly snug wool coat now wrapped around my shoulders.

Erron plucks the champagne from the ice bucket and points the slender neck of the bottle at Cole. "You just happened to marry the only half-demon witch in existence?"

Cole retrieves his pants from the platform and slides them up his legs. "I read the curse on her back and figured out what she was before she even knew herself."

My brows furrow. "You want a medal for that?" I snap, half joking, half not.

Erron chuckles at my outburst. "I like her. A half-demon...might work."

I size up the old warrior again. "There's a legend that fallen unicorns can be brought back to life."

He rubs the deep crow's feet near his eyes. "Unicorns are peculiar creatures. They live for duty. For the good of many. No wonder they are almost extinct. The mermaid songs were a pretty metaphor for a long-forsaken, beautiful ritual. It's a folks' tale, nothing more. Elisheba is gone."

"What kind of ritual?" Cole asks, sharp interest rising at the end of the sentence.

Erron gulps down another swig of champagne. "Nothing can bring someone back from the dead. Not the most powerful sorcerers in your realm—and certainly not Fae princes..." His gaze darkens, and he slams the empty bottle on the table, hard enough to crack it in two. The loud clink of broken glass tears through the air. "Enough pleasantries. Where is the horn?"

21

AFTERLIFE

Jules

"We should discuss this." I skitter closer to Cole. My bare feet leave a wet trail on the polished hardwood floor. Blood-orange clouds filter the sunset's dim light into the lodge.

"He's my uncle. I trust him." He barrels ahead without touching me, a first since we got married.

"He tried to skewer you." I pat down my chest again to make sure my clothes are properly placed, still embarrassed that this mountain of a man saw me naked.

"He had his reasons."

I steal a glance at Erron. "Everyone wants the horn. What does it do?"

"It's not about what it does. It's about what it contains," he clips.

His grumpy answer justifies my fears that the horn isn't just a horn.

"Beth's soul is still in it," I say.

Deep lines crease his forehead.

My heart gives a hard thump. "I'm right, aren't I?"

He inclines his head. "Unless we free it properly, Elle will waste away in her bony prison."

Cole leads us to the magic vault in his room and retrieves a square-shaped black box. After he pricks his thumb on a small, needle-like fixture by the crease between the box's top and bottom, the lock clicks open. Cole unveils the horn with great care and respect. The velvet shroud wrinkles in his tight grip.

The shredded part where the bone was cut flips my stomach.

Erron's jaw clenches, the tremble of his lip visible for a second before his ineffable mask returns. "What a mess."

He turns to Cole. "Elle was a pro, and she had few weaknesses. Tell me every detail you remember, no matter how small it seems."

Cole rests a hand on the closest bed poster. "When I arrived in the garden, she was unconscious, but still in her human form. In my altered mind state, I could barely feel a thing, let alone decide anything. I just had this...urge to kill her at any cost. I was nothing but a mindless puppet." He spits out the last part, eyes glued to the floor.

Horrified by the toll such memories must have on him, I close the distance between us.

He skirts away from me. Not so suddenly that it's obvious, but the inches of deliberate space clue me in that he wants to avoid PDA in front of his uncle. "I suspect Osbourne managed to neutralize her and left her ripe for the kill, though I'm not sure how."

"Who is this Osbourne?"

We recount every detail of Oz's life we can recall, but silently agree not to mention that Oz and Beth were dating. While we argue about tiny bits of the timeline, my nerves whip into a frenzy.

Cole dumps a fresh log in the fire. "I stole Oz's file from the office. He arrived in Dark Falls around the time Jules' father graduated. He was a good student, but not the best, and he almost got expelled for the illegal trade of dragon scales on campus."

Erron rubs his stubble. "His surname rings a bell, but dragons are pretty recluse. I never heard of a dragon teaching at Dark Falls before. Is he an air dragon?"

"Definitely," I answer.

Erron growls. "That must be it, then. Beth's blood was an excellent conduit, and while that allowed her to use or sometimes shape other people's magic, lighting, thunderstorms, and high-voltage electricity could overcharge her."

I play with my fingers, adding to the discussion whenever Cole misses an important detail, but my mind is somewhere else. I brush the tiny scar on my elbow, left there by Allie's magic during puberty. Dad used to call her his little thunderbolt. I was the fireball, of course. We destroyed quite a few crown moldings and windows.

Erron slides closer to me and gives Cole a pointed look. "Give us a minute."

Fuck, I hope I didn't let the worry shine on my face. He can't know about Allie, not the Fae vigilante with a skewer the size of my arm.

Cole grits his teeth. "Whatever you have to say, you can say in front of me."

"Elisheba was the love of my life, and if she discussed my existence with Julia here, I wish to hear the details. Give an old man some space. I promise to return your scandalously *mortal* princess in good health."

Our gazes cross, and I give him a small nod. Cole grumbles but walks away.

After he's gone, I cross my arms around my chest. "You don't really want to discuss Beth, do you?" Why would an immortal Fae royal want to gossip with a witch who knew his ex for five minutes? It doesn't make sense.

"No. I want to discuss Colden, but I couldn't tell him that, could I?" He offers me his arm.

We walk a few paces toward the center of the house.

Erron clears his throat. "My nephew is attractive and powerful, but it's his mind that sets him apart from his siblings. He doesn't think like most Fae. He sees beyond what others reflect upon him."

He guides me to the library. "He's no fairytale prince. He's mightily ambitious. He can be downright cruel at times—and impossibly pigheaded."

I crinkle my nose. "You don't have to tell *me*."

The burgundy stacks gleam in the twilight. The warm sunset plays with my eyes and creates mesmerizing optical illusions, as though rows and rows of ancient books are actually on fire.

"Cole is the most infuriating man I've ever known."

"He wasn't meant to marry you. As small-minded as it sounds, this...*fling* could hinder his destiny and destroy his chances to become King," Erron admits on a sigh.

I glide my fingers along the closest row of leather-bound books written in Fae script. Their gold titles spiral at the edge of my vision. "All because I'm mortal?"

"Mortal *and* half-demon. If you hope that this realm will look kindly upon that, you're mistaken. And you're too young to know what you really want. Cross-realm marriage is strongly discouraged because it almost always ends badly. Our culture, customs, and social cues are different. Most people from your realm can't wrap their minds around our way of life, what makes you believe you can?"

I slide a Fae dictionary from the shelf. "I'm willing to try." I'll start by learning their native tongue.

Erron steals the book from my hands. "How do I know you won't turn on him?"

I hold his judgemental stare. "You can't. Just like I'm not sure you won't kill me now."

Erron returns the book. "You're a realist. Elisheba was, too."

Beth meant a lot to this man. I clutch the dictionary to my chest. "Beth told me she should have married you, but that immortality got in the way. I think she'd root for us."

A tight breath squeezes past the full lips of the old warrior, his amber stare angled to the ground. "Alright... I'll support this marriage. Might help you two make it through the month."

After my discussion with Erron, I find Cole and Flynn sparring on the grass, down the steep hill, and I hide in the shadow of the building to observe them. Despite the rumble of the stream, their voices rise with a crystal-clear pitch.

Cole disarms Flynn with a quick blow to the wrist. "You're rustier than a witch's cauldron."

The sword tumbles down the hill.

Flynn rolls out of Cole's reach and retrieves his weapon. "I was stuck at the Academy with your girlfriend."

"Wife," Cole corrects him.

Flynn crouches into a fighting stance, now several feet downhill. "I'm not saying that word. It's blasphemous. We vowed to remain single forever, or have you forgotten?"

"We never made a formal deal."

"Don't I know it." Flynn's blade meets Cole's in mid-air with a loud *clank*. "Whatever happens, I'm not going back to Dark Falls."

Cole lets his sword fall at his side. "I told you not to visit your family. Grant always leaves you in these moods."

Four sisters and no parents... I wonder what Flynn's family is like.

The blond Fae takes advantage of the situation to regain the high ground. "Grant reminded me of my duties. Unseelies breached the wall in Thurst and cherry-picked their victims like it was a game."

A tremor slices through me, my ears and heart cold at the memory.

Cole buries the end of his sword in the earth. "I'll speak to the King. He'll send reinforcements to your brother-in-law. You're not going to the front." He runs down the slope and gestures for Flynn to follow.

The blond Fae climbs uphill instead. "There's nothing you can do to stop the war, *your highness*. As long as the Unseelie encroach on your lands, people like me will die to protect the borders and our people. This is how the world works."

Hands tucked behind my back, I flatten my body against the wall, the nook of the balcony still shielding me from their view, at least for now.

Cole dashes up the stairs and clutches Flynn's elbow. "Infernal magic kills Unseelies. I need some time to figure this out. You're not going."

Flynn's nostrils flare, and he shakes himself loose in one quick, unapologetic motion. "You don't get to make decisions for me anymore."

Cole lifts his chin. "Are you really going to risk your life to spite me?"

"You've got some nerve..."

A nasty right hook slices the air, but Cole ducks at the last second. Flynn throws another punch, his fist colliding with Cole's side. This is no longer a training exercise.

Cole spins around and gives his friend a forceful push.

Flynn staggers off to the side, but manages to stay upright. He expands his chest. "Oh, let's go." With a vicious snarl, he leaps into action.

Cole deflects another series of blows. Despite their obvious skills, both men grow breathless. Their impressive speed quickens my pulse.

Impatience builds in the bend of Cole's brow. "You moron, picking a fight will not change my mind."

Beads of sweat pearl on Flynn's neck. "If you order me not to go, I'll raise hell. You're married now...don't hold me hostage."

Flynn summons a dimensional ring and attempts to surprise Cole from behind, but quick footwork allows my prince to immobilize Flynn in a rear chokehold. The arm braced around Flynn's throat flexes hard, and the blond scratches at it with wide eyes before going limp.

Cole presses even harder. "Are you done?"

"Yes."

Cole inhales deep, his steel grasp unwavering. "Punch me again, and I'll throw you in a dungeon for a few days. That ought to bring some sense back into you."

With a growl, he releases his friend.

Flynn twists around to face him. "I haven't seen you with your panties in such a bunch over me in quite a while." A hollow shade of bitterness colors his face, but he doesn't walk away. Instead, he steps one leg between Cole's and crushes his lips to his.

I expect anger. I expect jealousy. Anything but the boom in my chest and the red-hot, desperate ache in my belly. When I saw Cole kiss other girls at the Academy, it made me feel small and stupid. Seeing him kiss Flynn is different. Maybe because I also kissed Flynn —maybe marrying Cole made me more like the Fae than I realized.

Cole firmly pushes Flynn away. "I love Jules."

My insides turn to mush. A ball of fire and nerves burns my windpipe. Love. He never said it to me, and yet the way it flows so easily out of his mouth steals my breath.

"I know, " Flynn grits through his teeth. He doesn't seem surprised by Cole's candor. "It doesn't have to completely erase us."

"She's an *earthling*," Cole answers. The word doesn't quite sound dirty, but apprehensive—and full of judgment.

"She would still love you."

Cole pats down Flynn's back in a soothing manner. "The prudish ways of humans have molded their views of our people and crystallized their prejudice... I will stay loyal to her if that's what it takes."

A sad smile glazes over Flynn's lips. "How could she not love you? I never seem to be able to stop, no matter how difficult you make it."

Cole squeezes his shoulder. "Come on, Verinos. Don't force me to play the prince card. Give me a few more weeks. If you still want to leave then, I'll let you go."

Flynn rolls his eyes. "Alright."

They head back down the stairs, and I tuck my curls behind my ears. A few feet more, and they would have caught me red-handed.

Cole and Flynn have history.

It was palpable in every angry spat they shared and every envious gaze Flynn ever sent my way. Written on that damn stela they used to communicate and in the bob of Flynn's throat at our wedding. They were friends, colleagues, and *lovers* before I came into their lives, and while that intimacy should threaten me—it doesn't.

Cole's offer to let Flynn into our bed still burns at the tip of my ears.

Hearing them discuss my *prejudice* infuriates me, but it's also disarming. It forces me to reconsider so much of what I thought I knew about relationships.

Fae are bad. Lust is evil. Don't let the big bad Fae wolf bite little Red-Riding Jules, or she will follow him to his world and abandon her family. Grim fairytales served as the base of my knowledge on an entire world and its people.

I can see now how plain wrong that is.

Cole's declaration softens my knees.

I only wish he trusted me enough to make up my own mind.

THE FATED WOLF

Allie

The white room at the top of the stairs in Daniel's new office building traded Fae royalty for dust and spiders. The eight-legged, hairy creatures scatter in the cracks below the desk.

Magisterium officers ransacked the desk and tore through Cole's belongings, leaving behind only the inconsequential. I'd hoped I could find clues in the mayhem, breadcrumbs to follow my sister's footsteps.

The prince of Faerie used to sleep here, on the expansive bed—along with the long string of girls he seduced. On the day I arrived at Dark Falls, the Fae prince favored Brie, his life-long friend. A month later, it was a panther shifter, and the month after that, his Fae-sanctioned girlfriend, Jessa.

When he laid eyes on Jules and claimed her as his teammate, I knew that meant trouble. Trouble for Daniel and I who planned to root out the Fae from our realm and strip them from their toxic influence, but also trouble for the Winslows.

My family's reputation will not survive another scandal.

I run my fingers along the bedspread, a thick Faerie fur the only tangible remnant of his presence here, and sigh.

Dan cracks the door open. "Are you still in there?"

"Ugh."

He wraps me in his arms. "You can't visit Jeremy Byers again."

I let my head fall on his shoulder. "Why not?"

My dragon is a jealous man.

He squeezes me tight. "His fever is not a fever at all. He's got a hollow inside him."

"A hollow? What's a hollow?" I spin around to face him, and the grim curve of his mouth spells out the seriousness of the situation.

The gentle kiss he places on my forehead should soothe me, but I secretly hate how he uses this particular caress to highlight my lack of knowledge. I'm eighteen—he's not. I hate to be reminded of how much experience and skill he holds over me, how doomed our relationship is if the truth comes to light.

"Hollows are ancient creatures we thought had been sealed away for good. They can't be killed or extracted once they're buried in a host, and they use their prey to replicate," he explains.

I dry my clammy hand on my skirt. "Are you implying—"

"Jeremy's suffering is coming to an end. Tonight."

I flee from his embrace, stunned. "There must be another way. We can't just kill him." Not him, too. I keep the last bit to myself, knowing how touchy my Oz becomes when I mention Miss Eillis.

His lips curl down. "There's nothing else we can do. The thing took root inside him. If we let him live, it'll suck part of his soul out, and that fragmented part will become a hollow, too."

I press a hand to my mouth to suppress a horrified grimace. Jeremy. My first boyfriend at Dark Falls will not live long enough to finish his first year...We weren't right for each other, but I hardly imagined this.

"It's a mercy. I hope you understand."

"I do." I'm not dense. If Jeremy can't be cured, letting the hollow have his soul is not an option, and yet, my skin tingles. Daniel is hiding something, I'm sure of it.

His arms fly around me again. "It could have been you, kitten. You can't fly around in the forest alone anymore."

I tie my long blond hair into a ponytail at the back of my neck. "I want to come with you tonight and help Jeremy if I can."

No one should be alone when they die.

Dan shakes his head. "He's incoherent by now. You don't have to see that. Let me deal with it."

"I want to be involved. I told you before—I'm not cut out to be an ornamental wife. If we're in this together, then I want to help."

"This is different. It's official High Council business. You can't tag along. One day, we'll be free to share everything, but until then, we've got to be careful. Promise me you'll go to bed and try to sleep. You have exams coming, and we can't afford to let down our defenses, not even for a minute. The trial will go on."

The trial...

After Jules' disappearance, we asked for a continuance. The respite was brief.

I press my hand to my brow, a migraine threatening to burst between my eyes. "I can't believe Cole double-crossed you and refused to give her back. I hope she's okay."

Dan rubs my upper arms. "Hey. I'll do everything in my power to get her back. You have my word."

A tingle of lightning between my shoulder blades distracts me. I can't help but feel he's holding back information, and my powers rarely mislead me. I watch his retreating back and head to our bedroom.

Despite my promise, I change into my black hoodie, wrangle a pair of dark leggings over my nylons, and slip into the night.

The infirmary is perfectly visible from the forest. I climb up a tree until I'm at eye-level with the second-story windows. From this angle, I can almost see into Jeremy's room. Shudders quake my arms and chest, but to my surprise, Dan and his agents walk in and out of the building in minutes.

When they step on the gravel in front of the dining hall, Theodore Darkwood is with them.

A blue aura gleams around the President of the three realms. A powerful magic armor, no doubt.

A levitating stretcher glides in front of them, controlled by Daniel's magic. The agents fan on each side until the procession reaches the line of trees. Darkwood motions my boyfriend along, and they enter the woods—where I'm currently hiding. Fuck.

There's really only one place they could be going, so I hurry ahead of them and choose my vantage point carefully.

I perch on the high branch of a thick, powerful oak. The serrated leaves encumber my line of sight, but there's no way they'll be able to spot me. The wind blows square in my face, so my scent shouldn't reach Darkwood's vampire nose.

The underworld tear has grown since I last saw it. It used to be inches long, but it's at least six feet wide now. The shadowy margins snake along the rocks before they disappear inside the flat stone slab, where the portal leaks deeper and deeper into Dark Falls' roots.

The stretcher comes into view first.

Then Dan.

Darkwood closes the funeral march.

The blue armor around him glitches when he steps past the stony ridge where the unnatural rock slab begins.

I drag my parched tongue against the roof of my mouth.

When the stretcher is but a few feet away from the tear between worlds, Dan raises one hand to Jeremy's head. An acrid yellow glow flashes in the night. The pine needles around the clearing squirm at the burst of power.

My dragon dumps the body inside the portal the way I dispose of the dead hair on my comb.

My heart pounds in my throat. Jeremy is dead. Just like that. And neither man will lose a night's sleep over it. I bite down on my tongue, hard enough to draw blood.

I can't cry. Not here. Not now. Not ever.

If I want to play in the big leagues, I have to toughen up—only, this mercy kill feels everything but tough. Jeremy didn't deserve to die alone, toted through the shadows like nothing more than a sack of potatoes.

Both men stroll away from the gateway and closer to my hiding spot. I hold my breath.

A perfect shimmer envelops Darkwood again. For whatever reason, his armor didn't function properly close to the tear.

Dan stops at the edge of the clearing. "The portal needs to be closed."

Darkwood forges ahead. "We can't speak of this now."

Daniel intercepts Darkwood as he doubles-back on the trail and forces him to slow down. "Last time we faced the hollows, we had to give them fifty souls to trap them. We can't let that happen again."

Goosebumps tingle up my arms.

Fifty souls? How can that be? Unless they used humans, fifty magic-attuned citizens haven't gone missing since—

"We haven't got fifty students to spare this time around," Daniel barks.

Darkwood remains as silent as his empty soul.

Oh Gods.

Four dozen students died in their sleep about a year after Dad graduated the Academy. Witches, seers, warlocks, and necromancers...all mortals. They'd never found the culprit, but, if I'm understanding this right, the investigation had been all for show.

Electricity buzzes in my palms, and I ground myself to the tree's trunk not to spark off into a storm and attract their attention. *But Daniel was a student then, he couldn't have been involved, could he? They probably filled him in when he became headmaster. He must be freaking out as much as I am.*

"We have to act now."

"We?" Darkwood cracks with a flash of teeth.

Daniel inches closer to the president, his lips curled back in warning.

Sparks lash through the space between them in a flurry of colors.

"Don't forget yourself, Osbourne. Or you won't be the wizard of this school for long."

The nerve! If it wasn't for us, he wouldn't be President.

I read the same call for justice in my dragon's eyes, but he quickly bows his head to cover up his anger. The rap of his fingers on his thigh betrays his impatience. "It will take us months to fix a tear of this size. We need help." He angles his chin to the tear between worlds. "We need the witch."

I bite my lips.

"You fool! We don't need a child—"

"Beth was the only one of us who knew how to close the damn portal, and you ordered me to kill her." Dan grounds out, his entire body stiff. "I'm positive she taught Julia Winslow how to access her powers. If you don't want a mass grave to be dug on your watch, the infernal witch is our only hope."

I take solace in the fact that, despite all the classified information, my dragon was honest about his desire to find Jules and bring her home.

But I don't trust Darkwood, and I wish my Oz didn't need Jules' powers for a dangerous mission.

Most importantly, I wish he didn't need her magic more than he needs mine.

23

WRITTEN ON THE BOX

all blueish-gray pines flank the stables at the back of the lodge. I'm pleased to find the gentle brown mare there in the morning.

When Flynn mentioned he'd brought her along, I couldn't resist the urge to ride.

Her coat shines in the bright light, her ears straight as she prances proudly toward me. She's all dolled-up in her royal colors, her mane braided with copper and silver threads. The black bridle hanging from her box's door is polished to perfection.

I pass the halter past her ears and pet her neck. "What am I going to call you? Brownie?"

The mare blinks.

"Geraldine?"

She stomps the ground impatiently.

"Bay?"

She rubs her nozzle on my hand.

"Alright, Bay it is."

"You're such a cliché," Flynn says on a coarse whisper.

I jolt upward, spooked. "Fuck—you scared me. I thought I was alone."

The Fae leans one shoulder against the neighbouring box, his arms crossed. "Well, I'm here, too. You're not the only one who loves to ride."

My brain struggles not to fall down the gutter. After the scene I witnessed yesterday, I'm rattled. Are we enemies, vying for the same treasure? Or allies by association, forever stuck with each other?

The dapple gray gelding's coat drips with sweat, so I figure Flynn got up at the break of dawn.

He tucks his horse inside the box and feeds it fresh hay. "Or do I need to ask *her highness* for her permission to exist?"

I haven't been alone with him since our cross-realm adventure, but this sudden burst of ire catches me unguarded. "You're in a mood."

Does he resent me for Cole's choice?

He goes through the motion, his white-blond hair longer on one side, the fresh cut expertly disheveled.

"I thought you and I had found common ground," I say.

Flynn huffs. "You've barely said a word to me since we arrived."

Fuck, he's right. Between all the Erron drama, the Fae books, the scorching sex... I haven't really spoken to Flynn in days. I choke on an apology, my instincts screaming at me not to show my underbelly to Flynn Verinos, even if I'm in the wrong.

I clip Bay in the alley to saddle her up.

When I turn around to get her bridle, Flynn looms, his face inches from mine. My shoulders hitch.

A white shirt sticks to his golden skin, and the V-neck of the Fae cotton allows me a glimpse of his tattoos and leaves his forearms bare. The ocean in his eyes rumbles with barely-veiled grievances, but for a moment, I think he's about to lean down and kiss me.

"I knew you were there," he breathes instead.

The heat of his body seeps through the space between us, and I curl my fists. "Err—What?"

A grin tugs at his lips, but the joy doesn't quite reach his eyes. "I wanted you to see. We're past false pretences, you and I."

A hot breath flutters down my neck, and goosebumps freckle my chest.

He arches a brow. "Aren't we?"

Bottom lip tucked between my teeth, I nod.

Flynn slips Bay's bridle on with expert hands and throws a blanket over her back. "Cole thinks you're the same as the other mortals. Boring and closed-minded. I think you're better."

The back-handed compliment throws me for a loop. The throaty drawl is both a dare and a confession. It's intimate. I find myself entranced by the sight of him saddling up my horse, each confident move full of care.

Shivers scatter down my spine.

When he's done, he smacks a fool-hardy kiss above my ear, fingers tangled in my curls. "I'll be good and bide my time, but don't pretend you haven't thought about it."

Heat licks my ribs, my flames rising to the surface. Does he believe I'm the weakest link? That I'm his way back to Cole? Better yet, am I doomed to give in?

A WIDE AND pleasant trail snakes toward an emerald-green river. Thick oaks and petulant brooks forged their way into the rock bed. Fallen leaves crack underneath Bay's hoofs. We ride together at a lazy pace for about ten minutes before the bird chirps stop abruptly. The trail widens here, a few tall rocks laying at the bottom of a steep slope.

A shadow moves between the trees, and my shoulders tense. Cole assured me Unseelie creatures couldn't reach us here, the borders of his lands patrolled by royal guards. But then again, he also mentioned the monsters popped out of new areas every day.

Bay walks backwards and shakes her mane in alarm.

"Woah. Steady."

She spins around.

My head collides with a low-hanging branch, and the spooked horse starts galloping back the way we came. I grip her mane and lower my body.

Zzzsh.

An arrow—a fucking arrow that looks pointy as hell—wizzes by my face.

Zzzsh. Zzzsh. Zzzsh.

I crane my neck around to glance behind me.

One arrow buries deep inside Bay's rear muscles, and when I look in front of us again, my stomach churns.

A white horse blocks our course.

Bay's front limbs rise high in the air.

I roll to the ground, pain exploding across my nerves.

I cough up a mouthful of dirt and crawl to my knees, too dizzy to stand up yet. Magic swarms my body. Purple veins creep up my hands and arms. A perfectly formed purple orb crackles in my open palm, and I clamp down the urge to hurl it at the knight.

He recoils at the sight of it. "Where's your fire, witch?"

"Surprise!" I spit at the Fae.

Ten or twelve soldiers catch up to my rear, each of them holding swords. They prevent me from escaping, but they keep a safe distance, and quite a few of them steal glances at the purple orb.

The leader might be the only one that can use magic.

A leather strap runs diagonally over his chainmail, holding his quiver tight against his shoulder blades. The bow hangs from the saddle's pommel. A blue-tinged barrier shimmers around him, no doubt a magical armor.

I keep my eyes riveted on the archer. "What do you want?"

Last time I unleashed my new powers, I had no idea what they could do, or if I might explode along with them. Now, I'm more confident. They better watch themselves; I'm done holding back.

The man nocks his arrow and draws his bow.

I hope infernal magic will blast right through the protective barrier, because if not, I'm dead.

Sweat sticks to my temples. My hands shake. The orb snaps from my hand and flies directly to the arm holding the bow. The infernal magic zooms past the magical armor and cuts right through the archer's wrist.

His arrow bites the dust, two inches in front of my knees.

A gut-wrenching holler booms through the woods. The man's intact hand claws at his severed limb. Blood splashes the white's horse coat, a deep red splatter marring its braided mane.

I jump to my feet and watch the others' reaction, nursing another infernal orb to life. Raw breaths heave my chest.

Swords rise in the air.

I'm not in the Dark Falls' duel ring, and even if I was, I can't summon ten orbs and fight all these men. I just don't have enough juice. After four or five, based on my training sessions, they'll be too small to inflict real damage. My only hope is to scare the rest of them shitless.

Using both my hands, I smear the magic and create a half-crescent arch to hold the backline at bay.

I've practiced this trick with fire, but never with infernal magic.

One soldier detaches from the herd. "We can't allow a human to masquerade as a Fae princess. You signed your own death warrant, mortal."

"You signed yours, I'm afraid," I bluff.

Purple lines twist the skin of my arms, and a powerful, all-consuming current expands the air. The soldiers freeze, their eyes wide with fear, and I know I've graduated from *annoying little girl,* to *viable threat.*

The arch prevents them from approaching, but my jaw trembles at the strain. Hot shivers shake my entire body, and a groan tears out of my lungs. I've never pushed myself this hard. Never. I mostly acted on instinct when I fought the peeling hag.

At Dark Falls, Duel was child's play. We had a referee, and rules, and I can't believe I ever fooled myself into thinking it would resemble a true, life-or-death situation.

The knight jumps to the ground. "Keep formation. She's mine to kill," he hisses, his face wrinkled with fury and pain.

He staggers forward.

He's young, young enough to be my age. His wound already started to heal itself, and he unsheathes his sword with his left hand. "You better hope the healers manage to reattach my hand."

I step back, the half-circle of infernal magic at my back creeping along with me. "Or what? You'll kill me twice?"

"I will do worse than that, mortal."

A shadow quakes the ground between us.

Black feathery wings blink in and out of view at Cole's back as he lands between me and the knight.

Words like "the prince" and "he's here" echo in the clearing, and many swords falter.

The leader snarls. "I have my orders, *your highness.*"

"Then you'll die with them." Cole snaps his fingers. I know what comes next, and I take advantage of the chaos created by his mirror images to draw every ounce of magic I have left and hold my arch steady.

"Kill the girl!" the leader shouts.

A metal arrowhead sinks deep inside my belly, as unexpected and vicious as the sniper that shot it. My incredulous gaze latches onto its shaft, sticking out of my left side, an inch below my last rib. Red dots pepper the helical feather fletching.

The deep wound oozes with slick, wet blood. My hands fly to the tear, and I lose grip of my powers.

With a sharp whip of thunder, the arch of infernal magic explodes into a flurry of tiny shards that bury themselves into the soldiers' throat, necks, and heads.

I feel every single one of them rip through skin.

The soft flesh.

The agony.

Bodies plop to the ground. A crimson wave streams down my leg and taints the fallen leaves. The infernal shards dissolve into the ether as I fall flat on my hands. The veins on my arms twitch angrily. My neck burns as the next arrow misses its mark and only nicks the skin.

Two survivors scamper off, but twin black-and-blue orbs crash against their retreating backs, and they bite the ground, too. The white horse sniffs the lifeless body of his rider.

An arrow sticks out of Cole's right shoulder, and he tears it out of his flesh with a grunt. My eyes search the trees for the sniper, but the branches are still and silent, the third arrow nowhere to be found. Cole spreads his wings wide and wraps me up from all sides, forming a cocoon of feathers.

"Don't pull on the arrow, or I'll bleed out before you can heal me." The throb in my gut worsens, and I press my lips together.

He grazes the skin above the gash. "But how can you heal if it's still in there?"

Mortal biology must be as foreign to him as the Fae reproductive tract is to me. The wound stings, the metal head embedded deep in my gut. An inch higher, and Cole would already be a widower.

Then again, I might not survive the trek back to a healer.

"Can you fly us out of here?" I breathe.

God, I sound like I'm dying. Am I dying?

Cole lowers me to the ground and cushions my head. The world spins, the blue leaves and red sky above melting into a swirl of purple. *Whoa.*

"Too bad…I always dreamed of flying."

My prince snaps the arrow shaft sticking out of my side. Amber flecks twinkle in his clear irises and anchor me to consciousness. "Hold on." He mutters words in ancient Fae that jumble together in my pain-filled brain.

The incantation soothes the burn, but it doesn't slow the flow of blood.

Deep lines appear on Cole's face. "Fuck no."

Wicked tremors prevent me from moving. Purple lines still dig into the skin of my arms. Darkness skitters at the edge of my vision, beckoning me to fulfill my mortal destiny.

A horse stomps near my head—is it the reaper's mount? I couldn't say.

I force my eyes open long enough to distinguish Erron's shape. Not the reaper then. Not yet.

When my heavy lids lift again, Cole is gone, replaced by his gruff uncle.

The ache in my belly melts down to an itch, like a million tiny termites are munching on my shredded kidney. A hot burn tugs at my gut when Erron slides the arrow out.

My next breath comes easier, the one after almost divine.

"Is it done? Is she okay?" Cole shouts.

"She'll live, but it was too close a call. She needs rest. Give the magic a minute before you move her."

"Hey, Fire Girl. Can you hear me?" He tucks my sticky, stained curls behind my ears.

I blink and marvel at the sight of my blood-stained, impeccable stomach.

Cole heals the nick on my neck. "I owe you a long, hot bath. Don't worry. You'll be good as new in a few hours."

"How did you know?" I ask, my mouth pasty and dry. Morning breath is nothing compared to the taste of imminent death.

"I was in the gardens when Bay came running. The arrow was self-explanatory."

Bay neighs close to my forehead.

"Good horse," I whisper, still too weak to sit but no longer fighting the darkness.

"This is my mother's work. I'm sure of it." He picks me up in his arms, and I'm glad to see that the debilitating pain is gone.

Erron winces as he takes in Bay's injury. "Amateurs. They didn't even shoot cleanly. Are they all dead?"

"The sniper got away," I admit. Twelve corpses stick out of the grassy patch. I wait for a sense of guilt to invade my chest, but none comes. Twelve men came to kill silly little me, and I survived. I feel...proud.

Erron seizes Bay's reins. "He fled, so he might not know you survived, yet. That'll work in our favor."

Is that what Faerie is really like? Forget the warm, mystical lakes and the breathtaking view. "We're at war," Celeste had said as she sold me out to Oz. "You will never see my son again."

I hadn't grasped the depth of her warning.

Erron ushers Bay into the building to work his healing magic on her, too, as Cole carries me inside the lodge. His right arm secures my thighs while the other snuggles my shoulder blades. He buries his nose in my curls. "I hate that you're mortal."

My heart thuds. "It was written on the box."

He inhales deeply, and I relax in his arms. I almost died today and killed a dozen men. The honeymoon is over, indeed.

He lays me down on one of the couches in the foyer and traces the shape of his ear. "I never thought she'd go this far, but now that she started, she's not going to stop. I have to speak to the King."

The quietness of his voice suffocates me. Whatever Cole feels about his father, he's not optimistic about this meeting. I'd say he's downright terrified.

The fatigued lull that had crept into my flesh is chased away by a new wave of adrenaline.

King Kirkan, the sixth ruler of the united Seelie court, is about as legendary as Zeus himself. He's been ruling for centuries, since his father died in the Dryad War.

My abs scream in pain as I sit up. I steel myself on the couch's armrest not to topple over. "I want to go with you."

"No." The withdrawn mask of the Fae prince transforms his features. His body grows rigid. The few feet between us stretch into miles and miles of secrets and half-truths.

I've encountered this hardened version of Cole at Dark Falls often enough to recognize the change. Back when we were nothing, or when he pretended to be interested in Allie to spite me, his eyes would dim in the exact same way.

We barely know each other.

Celeste had snickered that his father would *beat him bloody* for marrying me...

I cross my arms over my chest. "If you're going to speak about me, I want to be there. That's not negotiable."

Cole drags his gaze from the tip of my boots to the fresh purple curls stuck to my cheek. "You do not make the rules here."

"Your father is a ruthless warrior. If you go alone, he'll assume I'm just a stupid mortal that tripped over her own feet to marry his pompous son. He needs to know I'm not a coward, nor a fool, and for that, I need the chance to look him in the eyes."

The corner of his mouth quirks before he presses his lips in a thin line. "My father will judge you for the strategic advantage you may or may not be able to deliver. The only thing that will matter to him is how useful you can be to the realm. Are you ready to face that?"

He's measuring my resolve, but through his cold and calculated expression, I detect a hint of fear...and pride.

I give this Darth-Cole a curt nod. "I'm ready."

I can't lose the Cole I've discovered. The mischievous, considerate one that allows himself to be vulnerable in my presence. I'll fight to keep him, even if it means I have to make a deal with his jerk of a father—or the devil himself.

24

A CROWN OF NIGHT

Jules

The labyrinth of tunnels Mary guided me through before the wedding holds no mystical sway today. Healed from the arrow but sick of ambushes, I'm looking forward to this much-needed return to reality. Still, a tingle of fear sizzles up my spine at the prospect of meeting the Fae King.

Cole and I exchanged barely two words about his father. We eloped in secret, and while a million reasons come to mind as to why we shouldn't have, none of them really matters but the fact that we barely know each other.

Instead of heading down the slope to the chapel, Cole steers me through an uphill passageway. It opens to an interior courtyard, each of the walls erected around it taller than the eye can see. The set-up would be quite difficult to access—only most inhabitants of Faerie can fly.

A tree, maybe ten stories tall towers in the middle of the secluded garden.

Silvery mist hangs on its low canopy and creates rainbows over our heads as we walk closer to the trunk. Beyond the veil of colors, the moon shines bright. Heart-shaped leaves reflect the silver rays, but their underside is all black. The two-faced quality of Faerie's most-sacred tree casts a chill along my collar.

"The Hawthorn is sacred to this realm. The Fae King harnessed its power when he was crowned—as did each King before him—and so my father's magic is intimately bound to this place," Cole explains, his voice quiet with deference.

I peek around. "There are no guards anywhere."

"The Hawthorn guards itself. Anyone who wanders close to its bark without the proper credentials will wither on approach. If they do not turn back, they'll die on their knees at its roots."

Goosebumps tighten the skin of my arms. "And it doesn't apply to me if I'm with you?"

Cole spins my wrist around and traces the faded tattoo. "You're tied to its magic in your own right. The mark will disappear, but the Hawthorn will not forget."

We weave around a natural staircase formed by low-hanging branches and hike to the top of the tree. The fresh mist leaves a soothing kiss on my shoulder as we pass through it, up and up, until we reach a flat, circular space. Five main branches gnarl in sharp angles toward the starry sky. Each limb splits into five smaller strands, like human hands sprouting upward to lift the crown of the tree.

Aerial roots wriggle along the flat space and draw three concentric circles.

Cole motions for me to stay behind the line and threads forward. As soon as he steps in the middle circle, a terrible vibration quakes the tree. Leaves bristles from above, a few dead ones rustling at our feet.

We don't have to wait long.

A shadow stretches to a human-shape that slowly ripples into a man.

"Colden," a terrifyingly charming voice purrs.

"My King," Cole bows before his father.

The Fae King is a dead ringer for his son, and my heart speeds up at the mere sight of him. Power ripples through the air. Spikes of magic prickle the skin of my cheeks, chest, and arms.

A lustrous black mane flows down past the King's shoulders, slicked back behind his pointy ears, and the sharp angles of his jaw cut through my mortal brain. Red and gold patterns illuminate the dark gray tint of his skin, like tiny fireflies drawing murals beneath the dermis. The lines and nodes glow in sync with the blood flowing through his veins.

Sacred blood, my mortal soul whispers.

My legs shake at the sudden urge to kneel and offer him my life, body, and soul.

Despite the grandeur of the apparition, the King's body remains slightly translucent, like a ghost, and I figure he's more of a hologram, his magic allowing him to take *calls* from this location.

After half a minute of dreadful silence, the energy settles into something less foreign, but equally cold.

"Your mother was in a rage about you," Kirkan drawls out.

Cole offers his father a tensed smile. "She forgets that I'm no longer a child."

Kirkan's eyes crease at the corners. "What about me? Would you defy my orders, too?"

"You're my King."

It's not a straight answer, but it seems to please Kirkan, because he smiles. "You want your mother to accept this silly marriage, then?"

"I want her to vow not to harm my wife."

I step into the circle.

Cole balls his fists, but he does not look back.

The phantom's gaze shines with a flash of ire. "She's *mortal.*"

"Power is power," Cole says through his teeth.

Kirkan sniffs the air, and the tightness of his jaw eases. "Demon blood flows through her veins."

"Yes."

"She's infernal."

156

Cole gives a curt nod. "And by the will of the Hawthorn's roots, so am I."

A cold, proud grin tugs at the corners of Kirkan's mouth. "The witch shall live...for now. Let Erron judge how deep the wells of hell run in her veins."

Cole bows again, the set of his shoulders a bit more relaxed. He warned me that his father's angle would be selfish, but I didn't expect for it to resonate so deep inside my heart. Joke or not, the infernal magic was a deciding factor in Cole's decision to marry me.

The Fae King glitches out of view.

"He took it well, I think." I mask the hurt with a healthy dose of bravado.

Without a word, Cole whisks me down the tree, back into the tunnels to the entrance of the chapel.

"Where are we going?" I ask.

The sight of the obsidian stone dries my mouth, but there are no kinky ghosts spicing up the air, and Cole leads me past it to the back of the chapel, to a patch of earth no different than the other nooks and crannies. Cole dashes directly for the solid wall, which upon closer inspection possesses a rainbow-coloured gleam that catches my eyes at just the right angle. We both glide through the hidden doorway.

On the other side, the passage appears as solid gold, and the dissimulated room dizzies my senses.

Above our heads, a circular brick dome with perfectly round holes that let a bit of moonlight shine through reminds me of Ancient Greek temples. The hypnotic patterns created by the forced-perspective quicken my breath.

On the ground, a dozen portals are set in a circle around an elevated rock pedestal. Faerie alphabet signets are carved into the stone above each of the portals. The closest Fae-made glass mirrors only my reflection, and I walk up to it.

I graze the polished surface, surprised to find real glass under my fingertips. "They aren't active?"

"Not yet." Cole holds his palm up to the empty altar, and immediately, a crack forms in the fabric between realms, right above the pedestal. "A tear as big as this is easy to open. When I *zapped* out of Faerie, I came here."

"A well-traveled path between worlds can never be totally mended," I whisper, remembering Beth's explanation about the Underworld portal near the heart of Dark Falls' power.

"Exactly."

I check the portals again, each of them now betraying hints of the worlds beyond them. "Where do they lead?"

"To Earth. We call this place the Hall of Mirrors. The portals function as a series of magnifying glass, if you will. They allow us to travel from here to all these places, and from each of these places, we can create smaller, one-time-use paths to return through what we call Faerie's main channel." He points to the tear between worlds. "But we didn't create the main channel, we just built a castle around it."

I marvel at the eight-foot-high shimmer. "I've seen something like it before."

Contrary to the one Beth and I opened, blue-tinged margins frame a well-lit crack, and the void between them radiates with warmth. A soft heat glides along my cheeks.

"It's a big Seelie secret. The science behind the magic that allows us to travel between your realm and mine at will, as long as we are within range of the main channel's magic. We can bring people along, but we're not supposed to." He caresses the edges of the tear. "Nobody is supposed to know that anyone could have this, that we are *taught* how to use the channel. They need to believe it's a sacred power we're born with."

His poise hammers at my anxiety. The black linen shirt sticks to his chest and highlights each of his ridges.

"Why are you telling me?"

"If you've seen something like this before, it means Beth showed you the one in Dark Falls. The one that leads to the Underworld." He turns to me. "How did she open it?"

I scoff. "Why? You fancy a honeymoon in hell?"

He rakes his dark curls back. "Onyx was not the first demon to wander accidentally into Faerie. More and more lesser demons are being found stuck between worlds. Unseelie use these cracks, these anomalies, to bridge our defences and murder our soldiers and citizens. The King believes they asserted control of a similar hub in the underworld. One hub in Faerie... According to our ancient texts, there used to be one on Earth, too, but it was destroyed. It seems logical that a third hub, the one that allows the Unseelie to disappear from a losing battle and later pop back out on another battlefield, would be located in the Underworld."

Three hubs. Three realms. I've paid enough attention in History of Magic to believe it.

"We need to find a way to close these breaches. Either your mother came from one of these tears, or your father travelled to the underworld. How?" He encircles my waist, his hands resting on my hips.

I rap an absent-minded pattern on his chest. "Did you marry me for my magic, or my brain?"

"I love you for both."

My stomach squeezes, and I glance back at the main channel, the mother of all Faerie portals, and shiver at the pulse of power emanating from it. "You're only asking because you want to save your people?" Cole is many things, but an idealistic Prince Charming, he ain't. That much I've known from the beginning.

If I'm about to confess my undying love to him, I better do it with both eyes open.

"How can I become king someday if there's nobody left to rule? The realm needs infernal magic to get the upper hand on the Unseelie." He gives a rogue smile, full of cockiness and affection, a mix only Cole Desirys could pull off so beautifully. "I simply need *you*."

Love...need...Can he truly love and need *me* when he needs my powers more?

I squint at him, trying to see past the immortal prince to the man beneath. "Your uncle seems to think I've ruined your chances to become king."

Cole scoffs. "He had his fair share of *flings*, too. His opinion is skewed."

A smile creeps on my lips as I look up at my prince, his world domination speech not the turn-off I thought it would be. "You eavesdropped on our conversation?" I don't need his answer to know I'm right.

"One day, I'll be king." He presses me to him, our hips flush, his hand hot against my lower back. "And you'll be my queen."

I won't live long enough to see his father die, I'm sure, but the way he murmurs the words drums in my veins like a church's choir.

I might as well play along. "We'll start by freeing the courtesans, then, and offer mortals a real choice on the life they wish to live."

Our noses touch, and he leans in for a kiss. "Whatever you want."

He tastes a little bit spicy, a little bit dark…maybe even a tiny bit evil.

Eyes cast down, I straighten the lapels of his black shirt. "I love you, Cole. Even if I'm terrified to say it out loud."

He curls his hand over mine, his lids fluttering shut, the corners of his mouth curled up in a dashing smile. "Don't be scared, Fire Girl." His forehead presses against mine. "I'm yours."

It's silly, but in this moment—for an instant—I actually believe we could change the world. Cheers to young fucking love indeed.

25

HARD BARGAINS

Jules

The next morning, back at the lodge, I find Cole huddled with Erron on the balcony. The men stop talking as I draw near, and I eye my husband suspiciously. "What are you two talking about?"

The overcast sky presses the weight of the unending Fae summer on our shoulders, the barometric pressure through the roof. A tingle in my bones whispers that a storm is brewing.

"The Fae Solstice ball at the castle looms. In exchange for helping us, the King wishes us to attend," Cole says without meeting my gaze.

I shrug. "Fine. I want to go."

Erron brings a hand to his mouth. "You want to celebrate the Fae Solstice?"

I take my rightful place by Cole's side and stare down his uncle. "It's the most important Faerie holiday, isn't it?"

Erron takes his leave with a snarky smile stuck on his face.

Cole leans against the bronze bannister, his elbows propped on both sides of him. "Fae time is so fucked up, we can't exactly celebrate the New Year or anything like that. But once in a while, all the Fae time zones merge for a night, and the red sun doesn't set on the whole realm for an entire day. During the Fae Solstice, we celebrate the renewal of life by drinking and dancing all night. The red sun's magic also shines on couples who wish to have children. Fae are not very fertile, so it's the perfect time for—

I step between his legs. "Fucking?"

He grips my waist. "Lots of fucking. Around midnight, gowns will start to pepper the floors."

"Kinky Cinderellas."

Mischief dances in his clear, amber eyes. "You're not as freaked out as I thought you'd be."

"That you celebrate the holidays naked? Fits your reputation." I press my lips to his to punctuate my statement and skitter pass the corner of the wrap-around balcony.

Erron is walking down the hill to Flynn. The blond Fae trains alone today. I still haven't admitted to Cole that I eavesdropped on their conversation. I chickened out half a dozen times.

Flynn returns his sword to the table as Erron draws near.

I don't think I've seen them together, yet, and though Flynn's glamor shines as bright as ever, his serious pout unnerves me. He nods at whatever Erron says like a soldier accepting orders from his general.

Cole's brows form a thin line, and he jumps over the railing. "Go grab breakfast. I'll catch up."

I nod. Breakfast. That's another mystery I intend to solve.

Curious about the servants of the estate—who never make their presence known—I wander into the narrow stairway behind the library. Besides Mary, I haven't seen any servant, maid, or butler, but the floors are always shiny, and fresh clothes are neatly folded on Cole's dresser every morning. Magic might help with chores, but a Fae sorcerer would never waste his talents on housekeeping.

I suspect Cole asked his staff to remain invisible. I need to figure out why.

At the bottom of the stairs, a petite, delicate woman is cutting charcuteries and plating them on a marble island in the middle of the kitchen. A white courtesan's uniform hugs her tanned body. The dark, empty mouth of the wood-fired oven looms behind her. Large sinks are tucked in the back of the room. This lodge is fully-equipped for a royal feast.

The woman's shoulders hitch at my approach, but she continues to prepare the plate. Sequins glitter under the torches' light, and a gold belly-button ring shines on her bare stomach.

I walk to her and extend my hand. "Hi, I'm Jules."

"I know who you are, your highness." The words—as well as her entire demeanor— are stiff and tight.

I look at her once more. With her beautiful brown hair braided to perfection, and her Faerie-sun-kissed bronze skin, she's as beautiful as mortals come.

Did Cole use to sleep with her?

I grip the edge of the island, my knuckles white, trying not to care about the answer. "What's your name?"

"Iseult."

I draw in a deep breath. "Do you like it here?"

She doesn't quite meet my gaze. "It's an honor to serve the prince."

I fail to mask a cringe. "Answer me truthfully. Is being here your choice? Your desire?"

She deposits the knife on the cutting board. "It's my choice, but not my desire."

I get the feeling she would never speak so freely in front of the Fae, but I'm her peer, and the disdain she clearly has for my rise to fame works in my favor here. "How?"

"My family is poor. I have twelve brothers and sisters, and my position here assures them a future. When I first came to court, I was ecstatic, but the novelty of the glitz and glamor faded with time. I could leave, but then one of my siblings would replace me. Don't think I'm not grateful. I am. I was chosen, and I am content."

Despite Cole's claims, mortals that serve the Fae do have other ambitions in life. They're not slaves by the strictest meaning of the word, but they are stuck in the caste system. While I recognize much of the mortal world in Iseult's situation, it doesn't ease my anguish at her predicament.

Dad's position always allowed me choices that most mortals on Earth don't have. A privilege I often forget about because I didn't have to fight for it.

Still... Slaving away at a day job you hate doesn't feel the same to me as serving the every whim of Fae royalty and offering them your whole future—body and soul.

"Now, please let me finish my task in peace," she dismisses me.

Dad wasn't right about Faerie, but Cole doesn't see it exactly for what it is, either.

Flynn springs open the kitchen door. "Come. Now."

The urgency written in the worried curve of his brow pushes me into action, and I quickly dash over to him. "What's going on?"

"Trent is here," Flynn answers quietly, his eyes wide.

"What?"

"You heard me."

I run after him up the stairs to the library, and he quickly leads me to the main room, where two guards dressed in black and silver uniforms stand closely on each side of Trent Darkwood.

The vampire stands stiff as a statue, but his shoulders ease when I come into view. Cole waves away the guards with a dismissive sleight of hand and motions for Trent to sit on the velvet couch closest to the fire. Flynn sits on the opposite side and glares at him, his jittery legs distracting as hell.

Cole serves himself a drink at the bar. "How did you find us?"

Trent rubs down his face with both hands. Wet hair sticks to his pale skin. "This place is hardly a secret. Mel visited once or twice. My Dad used his connections to get me through to the nearby village."

Cole glares at Flynn.

The blond looks as guilty as a leprechaun with one hand still stuck in the cauldron. They stare at each other until my skin itches.

I force my attention back to our visitor. "Why?"

Of all the people I imagined might ride into Faerie to knock some sense into me, Trent didn't make the list.

"Let's not beat around the bush. My father needed to reach you." The vampire tilts his head back on the cushions, fingers pressed to his eye sockets. "I'm here because I'm...expendable."

What kind of father sends his son on a dangerous mission to Faerie without back-up? If Trent had been caught by anyone but Cole's guards, who knows what could have happened. Drenched to the bone, with his leather jacket and Dark Falls uniform, he doesn't exactly blend in.

Trent's arm slices through the space in front of him. "If you decide to keep me here, my father won't lose a night's sleep over it. That's the truth."

I brace my elbows over my thighs and munch on my thumb. "Why did he send you at all?"

"Dark Falls is under attack. Right after you left, hollows started to slip through an Underworld tear. If the portal isn't closed soon, they'll have to evacuate the grounds altogether."

"Hollows?" I check Flynn and Cole's faces for traces of recognition.

My dark prince downs his shot glass. "Hollows are ancient monsters that feed on people's souls."

"And why do we care? If they evacuate, great! Let them sweat," Flynn says.

I wet my lips. If the Underworld tear opened again... "What does your father want from me?"

"You can close the portal with infernal magic." His throat bobs. "Can't you?"

I walk away and stare out the windows. Small yellow birds quack happily in the trees. Sluggish rain beats on the terrace.

Beth showed me how to open and close the tear *once*. She didn't explain half the things that happened, nor tell me exactly how it worked, but I can't let that uncertainty show.

I spin around to face Trent. "Your dad needs a favor from me. I want one in return."

He nods. "I'm sure he'll agree if the terms are reasonable and make him look good to the press."

"I want a meeting."

The vampire approaches me. "If you come back with me, we can—

"

Cole dashes over to him, so fast I almost didn't see him move, and blocks his way, one arm firmly holding the vampire back.

The boys stare each other down, but Trent sits back on the couch, his nostrils wide, his crimson eyes pulsing.

"Not on Earth. Here." I turn to Cole. "Is there such a thing as neutral ground in Faerie?"

My prince twines our fingers, a clear show of ownership and testosterone. This is not the time or place to assert his superiority over Trent, but I allow it.

Cole bites back a growl. "My guards will take you back. Tell your father to meet us at the inter-realm checkpoint tomorrow at noon, Dark Falls' time."

Flynn clicks open his special watch. "That gives us a few hours."

"Alright." Trent awkwardly rubs his hand down his pants, and his gaze darts to where the guards were a minute ago like he expects them to appear.

"Come. I'll walk you out," I say without giving Cole the chance to argue.

The prince's glare prickles my neck, but I forge ahead and take Trent with me.

"The guards will be waiting by the gate," I tell the vampire.

He breathes a little easier once we're outside. The main entrance to Cole's lodge isn't well-traveled. The staff and visitors pretty much use the palace portal, but his personal guard patrols the perimeter.

The harsh rain gives way to a warm drizzle, and Trent pauses at the bottom of the stairs, near the life-size statue of a panther. The feline surveils the gates with its stony eyes, its back hunched like it's about to pounce. The statue resembles Onyx to a frightening degree, and I promise myself to ask Cole about it later.

Oblivious to my new discovery, Trent buries his hands inside his pockets. "You look…okay."

I frown. "Why wouldn't I be okay?"

He sways from the balls of his feet to his toes a few times. "I don't know…rumors, I guess."

"What rumors?" My eyes narrow. "We don't have much time."

"Oz told everyone you were…stuck here."

"That's ridiculous. I'm no prisoner."

He grabs my wrist. "Come with me then, back to Dark Falls."

I shake him loose. "In Dark Falls, your father is the President of the whole realm, and I'm an eighteen-year-old thief. I need to speak with him on my terms."

Trent shakes his head. "Be careful, Jules. My father will get his way in the end. He always does."

The rain intensifies once more. I pull the hood of my sweater over my hair. "Your father didn't send you because you're expendable. He sent you because we used to be close."

"Maybe. Still, he didn't know for sure I'd make it," Trent croaks.

We reach the gates, and the two guards from before wait alongside their colleague.

"Fucking fairies," Trent mumbles under his breath.

I cross my arms over my chest. "How's Lydia?"

"She's still upset about Jeremy, but—

My brows pull together. "Jeremy?"

Trent squeezes his eyes shut. "Fuck. I didn't mean to tell you like this. I forgot you didn't know." He covers his mouth with one hand, before he finally meets my gaze. "Jeremy is dead, Jules. He was killed by a hollow."

My heart beats furiously in my chest. "Dead?"

The soldiers notice our presence and close in on Trent.

"And more will die without your help." The vampire waves goodbye. A sad smile twists his lips. "Take care, Jules."

A crushing weight presses on my shoulders. *My* help. The realm needs *my* help to save innocents from ancient monsters, just like Faerie needs *my* infernal magic to kill the Unseelie. A meeting with the President of the High Council is as nerve-wracking as an interlude with the Fae King. If I'm not careful, I'll be swallowed whole.

I'm in way over my head.

THE INTER-REALM CHECKPOINT is nothing like I'd imagined. Airport customs came to mind whenever I pictured the infamously regulated hub where Fae, sprites, and pixies can officially enter our world. Small, illegal Faerie portals sprout in various places all the time, but regular Faerie citizens wouldn't want to be caught in our realm without their papers.

Long lines and bored magistrates don't exist here. There are no turnstiles, x-ray machines, or metal detectors. Instead, the checkpoint ressembles a spa, with white marble floors and a triangular-shaped fountain in the central plaza.

Three open-mouthed water dragon effigies spew water into the air. It cascades down many floors to a deep fountain at the bottom. Thin droplets stick to the glass banisters of the mezzanine.

No one in the crowd seems to mind the fresh droplets of water shining across their foreheads. Along the three sides of the triangle, many staircases head up to the floors above, each of them reserved for one particular species or merchandise.

Cole points to the sky. "The inter-realm portal is at the top. You head up the right staircase and meet with an agent before departing."

I skim the options. "There's no mortal signage."

"Mortals seldom leave Faerie," Erron remarks. Both men insisted on tagging along.

"Aren't they curious about their home world?" I ask.

Erron smirks. "Mortals in your realm have forgotten about magic. Most Faerie folks—mortal or not—find that distressing."

Cole pulls me aside. "Let's talk about this again. Hollows are extremely dangerous. Why would we stick out our necks and risk our lives for Theodore Darkwood?"

He's not happy with my plan, a fact he's made abundantly clear in the last few hours.

"Not Darkwood. If Dark Falls is in danger, the whole realm will be in jeopardy," I remind him.

"If hollows are drawn to power sources, like our research suggests, they'll hover close to the Academy. The Magisterium can put up barriers and restrict them to a small portion of the grounds—"

"It would not be a school anymore. It'd be a war zone. What happens when demons figure out the tear is active again? What then?" I say with an edge of sarcasm. The prince is stretching my patience.

Erron joins the conversation, indifferent to our efforts to speak privately. "The natural order of things is for the realms to be connected. When the Dryad War ended, after we sealed almost all the portals, the old leaders knew turning our collective backs on the underworld would come back to bite us, but they figured someone else would have to deal with the fallout."

The thin crowd becomes thinner still, and as the last traveller whistles out, two large doors open on the mezzanine.

Theodore Darkwood appears, flanked by eight Magus wearing black and yellow capes. I used to dream of working for the Magisterium, so I could have been one of them. Protecting a crook. An elected one, but a crook all the same.

A part of me needs to believe the whole system isn't rotten. Oz and Darkwood schemed meticulously to cover up their trails, so the Magisterium can't all be corrupt.

Cold, garnet eyes and a sharp salt-and-pepper beard polish off his well-trimmed, deadly look as he strolls down the stairs. The wrinkles on his face are filled with poise and secrets. This man probably hasn't had a spontaneous thought in a century, and his movements are crisp and purposeful like he planned them years in advance. Under his scrutiny, I'm a toddler with jitters. Undisciplined and wild, leaping from one direction to the next.

He expects me to throw myself at the windows like a frightened bird, and that might work to my advantage.

Darkwood barely acknowledges Erron and Cole, his predatory

gaze fixed on me. "I want to talk to Miss Winslow alone." He arches a brow. A one-on-one meeting with the President is a token of respect.

Cole doesn't move an inch. "You can't be serious."

I squeeze his arm. "I want to hear what he has to say."

My prince stiffens, his body immobile as a rock. I motion Darkwood to follow me to the closest bench at the bottom of the fountain. Water will drown out our voices while allowing Cole to keep an eye on me. I'm not naive enough to believe the vampire couldn't curse me somehow, given the opportunity.

Theodore Darkwood sits on the marble ledge and gazes up at the waterfalls, hands linked over his crossed leg. I sit next to him, a foot of empty space between us.

Water sprinkles his face, and he licks his lips. "I've always wondered about you."

He gauges me up and down. "Your father was nothing if not a shrewd, crafty politician. He knew what the stakes were in bringing you home. He could have adopted you under false pretences or placed you with a friend. He could have done a number of things that wouldn't have affected his career—and Piper's. But he chose to destroy years and years of hard work for a small, insignificant girl." He chuckles the last part like it's a joke.

"He did the right thing," I grit out.

"By you, yes. But his first daughter? His wife? If he hadn't had you, he might be President today instead of me. He had the power, the prestige, the panache for the job, but he gave it all up for you." Theodore strokes his pointy beard. "I wonder what he'll think when he sees how easily you succumbed to the enemies' wiles."

I swallow a hard lump. I wish I could tell him that Dad will be proud of me, that Fae aren't the enemy, but I can't fool myself.

"As President, I became aware of secret missions and the...special circumstances that preceded your birth. Winslow spent ten years in the underworld right before you were born." An evil glint flickers in his red eyes. "Tell me. Have you ever met your mother?"

I press my lips together. I can't confirm his suspicions, not in the slightest way.

"Ah! You already know. You're smart to remain silent, but I'm not fishing for confirmation. You're half-demon, Miss Winslow, and if I told the world, they wouldn't doubt it for a second."

I force a stiff breath down my lungs. "You hold all the cards, it seems, and yet, you need something from me." If he didn't, he wouldn't be making threats.

"The Academy is under attack from these spectres. The hollows threaten our lands once more, and I need to fix it."

I square my shoulders. "If I help you, I want Oz exposed for his part in Beth's death, and Cole exonerated of all charges."

He shakes his head. "I appointed Osbourne. It would make me look weak."

My pulse flutters. This is where I need to sell him hard on my vision. "No. You would be the genius that uncovered him. The one to crush a budding war with Faerie over a well-crafted lie."

His lips purse in contemplation. "The Fae would demand retribution."

"Let them have him, and the horn."

Darkwood scoots closer. "You've thought about this in detail." Despite his age and lean build, he could snap my neck before Cole or Erron could react.

I press the ball of my thumbs into the bench to keep from cowering away. "I did. As I understand it, I'm the only one who can close the portal for you."

If he'd had another option, he wouldn't be here. I'm banking on that.

He clicks his tongue. "They can have Osbourne, and your prince can be cleared of all charges. But I need the horn." He straightens his cufflinks and stands, adjusting the lapels of his suit. "Piper is sick. She needs its magic to survive."

"Then you will swear to keep my secret, and I'll meet you in Dark Falls tomorrow at midnight, Dark Falls time." I school my features into a neutral expression, but inside, I'm shaking. My heart soars. Allie helped kill Beth to save her mother. For the first time since I found out about her involvement in Beth's murder, things are starting to make sense. If we can free Beth's soul from the horn first, I might just be willing to give it back to them.

Darkwood extends his hand. "I swear it."

I glance at my prince. Erron stops speaking, and their animated chatter dies in one breath. "Not to me. You will swear it to Cole."

A flash of white teeth quickens my pulse before Darkwood snickers. "Well played, Miss Winslow. Well played."

26

SOLSTICE

Jules

Red, orange, and yellow vines with matching, freshly-cut flowers decorate the entrance to the palace's ballroom. Sinuous antler chandeliers float in the air, suspended by magic.

An incessant stream of enchanted bronze leaves topples from the ceiling and pepper our shoulders. Light reverberates off their polished shapes and dazzles the dance floor. A large banquet table in the back offers a variety of delicacies, from tiny tarts to an open-mouthed boar.

Women were asked to wear red, and the men black. I rebelled and wore a puffy red bolero over a black dress, along with ruby slippers that would have put Dorothy's to shame.

I already stand out, surrounded by flawless Fae glamors, with the prince on my arm... I might as well try to feel good. The tattoos on Cole's bare chest are visible, his jacket left unbuttoned.

"My sister, Helena, hosts this year, so she chose the theme. Thank the Gods, the last one was all togas and laurels." He adjusts his bronze cufflinks, and I school my gaze back to the buffet not to drool. Married or not, the sight of him all dolled up...

"Are all your siblings here?" I search the crowd for Fae wearing earrings, which I learned from my readings is a mark of royal blood.

Cole grimaces. "By the Dark Mother, I hope not."

We greet Cole's sister at the front of the ballroom. People stand in line to congratulate her on a job well-done. Fae, sprites, pixies, and a few supernaturals chat in small groups, the guest list lengthier than I expected.

An old woman with bright-green hair and tanned skin reminds me of Brie, and I point to her discreetly. "Is that Brie's grandmother?"

"Yes. Erron invited the whole family, but with the current political climate, only Brenna Demers showed," Cole whispers in my ear.

My shoulders sag. I can't believe it, but I would have loved to see Brie and catch-up on Dark Falls. Information trickles to this realm slower than a baby ghoul, no one even heard of the hollows on this side of the mirror.

It's our turn to greet Helena.

Her sleeveless, heart-shaped bustier barely covers her ample breasts. "You wore black." An edge chops through her melodic tone.

I tug on the lapels of my bolero. "*And* red."

Eyes narrowed to slits, she grins. "Are you a woman *and* a man? That would explain my brother's keen interest in you."

The wrath of a party planner should never be underestimated.

Cole smacks an annoyingly loud kiss on his sister's cheek. "Helena, fun party."

She twirls the cherry in her cocktail glass. "You should let me plan your wedding."

"We already had one," I clip.

"A *secret* one." She plops the plump fruit inside her mouth and snaps it off the strand. "You better hope father asks me to plan a legitimate ceremony."

Cole scans the crowd. "Where's—"

"Mother? You think she'd show up after the stunt you pulled? Went crying to daddy, did you?"

Cole pats her shoulder the way you handle an annoying kitten. "Always a pleasure, sis."

She leans closer to me, her glamor so bright and eyes so gold that I tremble. "So, little mortal. Are you a mouse, a spider, or a snake?"

I fight the urge to blink. "Are these my only choices?"

Helena Desirys scratches the skin of my lower arm from my elbow to my wrist with her long, stiletto nails. "The mouse will be eaten. The spider wove her web to entrap my brother, so she's patient and clever, but untrustworthy. The serpent seduced him, and will bite anyone who comes too close to her spoils."

I hold her intense gaze. "I'm a bull."

One corner of her mouth curls up. Her red nails fly up to cover the budding smile. "A bull?"

"Yep." I make a loud popping sound and forge ahead, leaving this macabre menagerie conversation behind me.

Cole snags a shot glass from a tray on our way to the back of the ballroom. He downs the liquid in one gulp. "Helena's a brat. She's my favorite, but she's not—"

"She's fine. I prefer banter to pointy arrows." I steal a macaroon from the delicacy table.

"About what she said…" He scratches the back of his neck.

The deep lines on his forehead and the crinkle of his nose bring me right back to his comment about prejudice and mortals. In the glitz and glamor of his palace, surrounded by his peers, Cole is the epitome of poise and self-confidence, but his sister apparently found the one flimsy button in his smug prince exterior. The button he secured with a safety pin, hoping no one would notice.

I raise my brows. "Aren't all Fae bisexuals?"

"Err—no."

Shit.

I bring a hand to my chest. "That was rude of me to assume. I just—"

He combs a hand through his dark curls. "Not rude. A majority of us are. But I thought it would...bug you."

"It doesn't," I say without an ounce of hesitation.

He arches a brow. "No?"

"No." I grip his collar and yank him down for a very public, indulgent kiss.

He allows it, and I don't care who sees us.

I've attended my share of Council parties. This isn't so different. There are no photographers, no press, no one scribbling notes in the corners, but world-class schmoozing buzzes in the clusters of courtiers. Most of them gossip in our wake.

A shroud obscures Cole's face when a new waiter presents me—and only me—with a tray of bite-size delicacies. Crystallized flakes glaze the breaded treats.

"Salt?" I ask.

"They pass these around to mortals to ensure their consent, though it's useless for you now."

"I wouldn't say that. It's tasty." I steal a few more before letting the waiter go, and quickly, my tongue itches with thirst.

A second waiter offers me a rainbow-colored cocktail. The glass is similar to a champagne flute, but without a stem or base, which is totally impractical if you want to set your glass down.

"What is that?"

Cole snatches the glass and holds it away from me. "Fae fine wine. You shouldn't drink it."

I huff. "Why not?"

He gives me a wolfish grin that's 99% condescension. "It's pretty strong."

It boils my blood, and I wrestle the weirdly-shaped glass from his hands and sniff the contents. The sweet scent of roses and chamomile washes through me as I take a sip.

I wince at the strong metallic bite, the wine full of blood and...tears.

Cole wiggles his eyebrows. "I knew you couldn't handle it."

An aftertaste of joy replaces the sting, and I drink another swig, careful not to choke on the thick liquid not to give Cole the satisfaction.

Once I've gulped it all down, I make an exaggerated *ah* sound and head to the dance floor, alone.

Cole is quick on my heels. "Gods, I love you."

A nervous hiccup interrupts my hip roll. "Oh?"

He whisks me up in his arms. "Forever."

My heels squeak on the ballroom's shiny marble floor as he deposits me back on my feet. He opens his mouth to speak, but grabs a more classic wine glass from an offered tray instead. His Adam's apple bobs as he tilts his head back and swallows the entire thing.

"Are you okay?"

Lines appeared at the corner of his eyes, and his breaths are slightly uneven—I might be crazy, but my instincts scream that something is amiss.

Cole holds out both hands. "Let's enjoy ourselves now before too much debauchery happens. We wouldn't want our solstice customs to hurt your witch sensibilities."

I snatch a fresh cup from the tray, too. Maybe I'm just Faerie drunk. Who knows what that might entail.

This red wine is more…straightforward. Booze and honey and sin.

"It's different. Tastes more like Faerie," I say.

He grabs a fresh glass from the server and raises it in cheer. "It's my favorite."

It's not at all like human alcohol. Music dances in my bones, and I'm light as a feather. The weird vibe I detected earlier melts, and Cole relaxes, too.

When a languid ballad starts, I hide my face in the crook of his neck. "I love you, too."

He caresses my shoulder blades, and we sway to the music.

The gazes glued to my back don't bother me until a familiar face appears next to us.

I haven't caught a glimpse of Jessa since the showdown with Oz, and yet, her ire is directed at me. Her red dress is almost see-through, her dark nipples visible through the thin fabric, her perfect curves on full display.

She twists my wrist around and sinks her black nails into the faint, discrete mark that's already half-faded. "Celeste made me swear not to tell anyone you eloped. If you're so in love, why does no one here know you guys are married?"

"It's private." I yank my arm free. "Let go of me."

Cole stalks closer to her, his spine straight as an arrow. "I was never going to marry you, Jess," he chimes casually, as though we're talking about the colors of the decor or the quality of the buffet.

Jessa releases my arm and inches back. "I didn't—"

A cruel smile stretches his lips. "My mother dangled me as an option for you to get you to spy on me in Dark Falls. Every single piece of information I floated your way, you relayed to *her*. Because of you, I had to watch over my shoulders every second of every day, all the while pretending to like you to appease my mother's suspicions."

Jessa's mouth parts in a silent, outraged cry. Her movie-star chin trembles with barely-contained rage. "We'll see if you still feel the same way when your *mortal* bride is old and wrinkly—or better yet, when her corpse rots in the ground."

With that, she spins on her heels and elbows her way through the crowd toward the exit.

Many members of Cole's entourage have their calendars marked for my future death. Too much champagne will flow at my funeral. Whatever happens, Cole will live most of his life without me, and my blood boils at the reminder.

I'm a mortal playing an immortal's game, and whatever I do, I'm going to lose.

27

ETERNAL FEVER

Jules

The Faerie wine has mostly left my body, but I feel restless. It's not like regular alcohol. It doesn't fog my brain, and there's no hangover in sight. Music seeps into the small alcove we took refuge in, reigned in by a spell.

I feel alive. Untouchable. Energy streams through my veins, my muscles coiled in anticipation, my senses crisp. The colors, scents, and tastes of the Seelie court dispense an equal dose of fear and excitement in my blood.

Jessa's jab festers at the back of my mind, but I'll prove to myself—and everyone—that I'm not dead yet. I don't need centuries to make my mark, and Cole and I might not last through the month, let alone the decade, so I don't have to worry about the fallout of a long-lasting, mortal-immortal relationship.

Fuck it, I'm going to have fun tonight and worry about my inevitable doom tomorrow.

"You're sure there was only alcohol in that cup?" I grin. "Do you add strength potions to your wines or—"

Cole presses his index finger to my lips. "Verinos is back. Wave him over."

Flynn passes in front of our hideout, and I stick a hand out to snatch his wrist, yanking him in behind the privacy curtains.

The dance rages on beyond the slivers of fabric. Bodies flash in black and red rainbows, and I comb my fingers through my hair while Cole catches Flynn up on the latest developments with Darkwood.

The blond Fae left after our meeting with Trent with a mysterious errand to run, which I'm sure relates to all the one-on-one, discrete exchanges Cole and Erron tried to hide from me. I'm a sucker for secrets, and I intend to crack my two Fae eggs open tonight.

Flynn paces the small space back and forth. "Darkwood has an angle. I can't believe you agreed to this."

"Hey, it was all her. I wanted to chain her to my bed for a few months." Cole's heated gaze glides along the grooves of my body.

I wrinkle my nose, and he smiles back with a sizzle that flips my stomach.

"We can't just trust Darkwood and hope for the best. We need to think three steps ahead. How are you so calm?" Flynn points an accusing finger at his friend. "We need to—"

I grasp his hand and squeeze it. "Calm down." My belly aches from the way he keeps saying "we."

A slow melody echoes through the ballroom. "Dance with me." I tug on his arm and drag him to the center of the secluded alcove. The Fae's hands are stiff on my hips, the distance between us awkward and uncomfortable.

I pause. "Don't you want to dance with me?"

"Yes." He finally relaxes and embraces me properly. His hands travel from my sides to the small of my back and brush the exposed skin.

A tight breath blows out of his mouth.

I peer over Flynn's shoulder to Cole, and my Fae prince is

entranced by the sight in front of him. I raise my brows, arms laced around his ex-lover's neck, and his amber eyes darken.

Flynn's lids flutter shut, and he presses his forehead to mine. "I have a bad feeling about this deal you made. Tomorrow's too soon. Darkwood will try to screw us over. You can't gamble with your life like that."

The protective edge of his voice trembles inside my heart. "Shush. It's a party."

"I don't—"

I press one finger to his mouth, the move straight out of Cole's playbook.

With a sigh, Flynn grips my wrist and kisses my knuckles with his eyes cast down. His hands shake. I didn't believe Cole when he said that Flynn was falling for me. I believe it now.

He's not *stuck* with me.

Overcome by the realization, I plant a tentative kiss on Flynn's lips, and he stumbles. The bully who couldn't stop yapping about courtesans and threesomes *stumbles*.

Doubts and champagne linger on his breath before he moans against my mouth, his kiss desperate and rash. With a steel grip on my hips, Flynn crushes me to him like he wants to fuse our bodies into one.

The forbidden Fae...the bully who led me here and offered me an apple. I might just take a bite out of him.

Cole lunges to his feet.

Flynn presses a hand to his mouth and skirts away from me. "You both know where I stand. I'll leave you two to untangle this—"

"Stay." I lace our fingers.

Flynn looks from me to Cole and back to our joined hands.

"Is that really what you want, Fire Girl?" Cole stalks closer, Flynn stuck between us.

Is that really what I want? Am I doing this for show? For revenge? I don't think so. Ever since Melanie planted the idea of Cole and Flynn in my head, I've thought about it. Even dreamed about it once or twice—dreams that always left me gasping for breath. The Solstice presents an opportunity to dip my toes in Fae waters. I have to leave tomorrow...life's too short.

"Absolutely."

"I'm game." Cole throws an arm around Flynn from behind and kisses his neck, gauging my reaction. My heart pulses in my throat, but whatever Cole sees pleases him, because the most devious smile stretches his full lips.

"Fuck." Shallow breaths rock Flynn's body.

Cole unbuttons the top of his black jacket with his free hand, one arm still wrapped lazily around Flynn, and whisks us away to the adjoining room. I unfasten Flynn's jacket and peel the fabric off him.

Cole slams the door behind us, shielding us from the music completely.

The prince quickly shrugs his jacket off, and I'm left standing in front of two toned, muscular, half-naked Fae. Identical symbols lick their collarbones and descend to the top of their defined abs, and I press my trembling hands on their chests.

Their heat softens my knees, and I swallow hard. Wild heartbeats echo through my temples.

I kiss Flynn again, hard enough to bruise him, acutely aware that Cole is right beside him. The knot at the back of my neck loosens, and I'm not sure which one of them untied it.

Cole caresses the back of my ear. "You want to see us fuck, don't you?"

Flynn and I both respond at the same time, "Yes."

The prince's eyes gleam with mischief. Was he talking to Flynn? I guess it doesn't matter.

"You heard her," Cole whispers against his friend's neck. "Kneel, Verinos."

Flynn falls to his knees between us. I shrug off the bolero. Flames scatter between my legs as Cole unlaces the dress' corset. Flynn reaches under the skirt of my dress and drags down my underwear. The scrape of his nails along my bare thighs untangles the knot in my throat.

My breasts are full and sensitive, and Cole tests their weight in turn. Fire sparks along my ribs, the heat so intense, I close my eyes for a moment. The dress shimmies off my body, and I step out of it.

Flynn turns his attention to Cole. He quickly works the prince's pants open and yanks them down.

When he takes Cole's length in his rogue mouth, my chest cramps with lust and need. The sight is so sensual, so risky, so destructive of all the acceptable, proper sexual behaviour that branded my conservative human upbringing that I can't help but stifle a moan with the back of my hand.

Cole desperately reaches for me and steals my breath with his kiss.

Flynn cups my ass with one hand and squeezes hard.

Fuck. Fuck. Fuck.

I shake as I draw back to breathe, entranced by the sight of Flynn's tongue running along the ridges of my husband's erection. His blond head bobs up and down, his cheeks hollowed out. I kick off my ruby heels, tempted to join him on my knees.

Cole grips Flynn's hair. "Enough. If we neglect her any longer, she will spontaneously combust."

Flynn plants a hot kiss on my hip bone, and I shudder as he stands up. Their tall frames cage me in. My breath stutters. They exchange mischievous, cruel gazes and turn me in their arms.

I'm back to that first day at school where I saw them for the first time. An angel Fae and a devil prince. A most primal part of me always desired to be worshipped by them both.

Flynn devours my neck, his chest flush against my back. My knees wobble, but he snakes an arm around my midriff to hold me upright as Cole drags one hand up my thighs. He strokes the tight bundle of nerves between my legs before sinking two fingers inside me.

"You're ridiculously wet, Fire Girl." Cole glowers, like he intends to punish me for liking another man's touch.

Flynn sneaks a hand between my legs to check his friend's claim and squeezes me tighter.

The prince chuckles. "And you... You're dying to be inside her."

"Yes." Flynn begs, the sound both hot and disarming.

The boys share a quick, almost violent kiss, and guide me closer to the bed.

"Lie on your back," Cole commands me.

"Don't order me around." I lick my lips but obey anyway, and a hot thrill spirals in my bones. The duvet is cool and fresh under my palms.

Cole snuggles in next to me and kisses my jaw.

A thin sheen of sweat glistens on Flynn's chest as he discards his pants.

Cole grips my right thigh. "Spread your legs."

I let my gaze slip from Flynn's face to his tattoos and down his sculpted body to his cock. It's not as thick as Cole's, but long and smooth. A blazing heat tears through my gut.

Flynn crawls over me, and the length of him bumps my inner thigh. I bite my lips as he sheathes himself deep inside me in one long stroke, and there's no pretending it's not the most wild and decadent moment of my life.

A dark glint flashes in the prince's eyes, and his jaw clenches as though he's about to wrestle Flynn off me and take his place. Jealousy mixes with arousal on his face, his brow bent, his bottom lip tucked between his teeth, his eyes full of envy and need.

After a few seconds, the cramped fist on my thigh loosens. Cole strokes my belly. "Squeeze him tight." His hand slides down to caress me, and my hips buck. Red lines of fire swirl at the surface of my skin.

"Fuck, that's hot." Flynn imposes a slow grind that totally disarms me.

Cole teases my breasts. "She loves to play with fire."

"She's perfect."

"She's mine," Cole barks, an edge of greed to his voice even though he's clearly more than turned on by the sight in front of him. He swallows my frustrated moan with a kiss.

It's too much, and I come hard with Cole's tongue deep in my mouth, and Flynn's cock snug inside me, my walls clenching desperately around him.

He gasps. "I'm not going to last long."

"I'm ready for her." Cole guides my hand to his erection, the tip wet from his arousal—and the insides of Flynn's mouth.

The blond Fae picks up the pace, the pinch of his face mesmerizing.

"I'll burn you both." I squeeze him tighter as I stroke Cole's cock. Both men hiss at the friction.

Flynn loses control, his release fast and messy. Sweat glistens on his tanned skin as he lays down beside me.

Cole flips me over his friend's chest. "My turn."

I collide with Flynn, overwhelmed, but Cole pulls on my hips with an impatient click of the tongue. Before I can fully brace myself for it, my prince enters me from behind, hard and deep. My knuckles whiten, contrasting with the black sheets. Flynn holds me steady. With a dangerous wink, he licks my left breast and traces the aureole with his tongue before sucking it inside his mouth.

Fire melts my insides, and I sink my nails inside Flynn's neck. Liquid heat leaks out of me as my body rushes to meet Cole's merciless thrusts. My lips part in surprise, but he gives me no time to recover between orgasms, his hands hard on my hips.

My husband molds me to his whims, exploring the deepest and most devious angles. I shatter in my lovers' arms, only to be glued back together by their gentle hands.

Soft, languid kisses on my shoulder. A wicked tongue in my belly button.

The legends might have warned me against the blistering Fae touch, but they never revealed the truth. I forget to scream, forget to breathe, ridden to such a blinding oblivion that everything but their scorching touch fades away. They exchange quick whispers and instructions, each of them dirtier than the last.

Tucked between my two Fae lovers, nestled in their heat and love, eternal servitude doesn't sound so bad at all.

28

IF YOU DARE

Jules

"Stay." Cole tugs gently on my arm.

I dig my heels into the stones of the hall of mirrors and stare at our entwined fingers. The event horizons of the secret passageways are already active, and the main channel shines in the Fae morning sun. Last night was…no word is strong enough to describe it, and I'll remember my first Fae Solstice for the rest of my life, but the time has come for me to return to Dark Falls. Reality awaits, along with scary, powerful monsters—politicians or otherwise.

A sad smile glazes my lips. "I made a deal."

"A human deal. There's nothing binding about it. Stay." His breath fizzes across my chest.

A white undershirt sticks to his skin, and the familiarity of the Dark Falls uniform twists my heart.

I play with the hem of my plaid skirt and bite my bottom lip. It's not like I can leave Dad, Lydia—even Allie—to the hollows. "Monsters are leaking into the realm. I have to help."

"Monsters leak into my realm every day. Help *me*." The ominous tremble of his voice gives me pause.

I search his gaze. "I'll do both."

"Darkwood gave up too easily. There's a catch."

"I'll be careful. Once your name is cleared, you can come back, and we'll finish the quarter together." I try to sound cheerful, but, hearing the words aloud, the possibility sounds at best like wishful thinking...

Cole scratches the back of his neck, his head tilted to the side. "Dark Falls won't take me back, whatever Darkwood promised you. It doesn't make sense for me to return."

"I know." I unfold his fingers and free myself. This marriage wasn't supposed to feel so real, and I can't help but fear it's coming to an end.

I rap my hands on my thighs, trying to summon the courage to actually step through the portal. "Alright, I'm ready. I just need the horn." My forehead creases as I realize Cole came empty handed. "You were supposed to get it from your vault. Where is it?"

He glares at the space between us. "I don't have it."

...

Cole wasn't on board with this plan, but I never thought he'd double-cross me. Never. Not after everything.

My chest contracts, and I force a stiff breath down my lungs. "Don't mess with me. Where is it? Did Erron take it?"

"The horn is gone," he says quietly, but with enough confidence to riddle me with adrenaline.

Fire swells inside my palms. "Gone—"

He brings a hand to the space between my breasts, the look on his face so peculiar that I freeze. Full of joy and yet...tame. "Your destinies were entwined. I think Beth chose you."

Chose me?

He tucks a curl behind my ear. "The ritual Brie's grandmother talked about was actually a spell to bestow Beth's gifts unto another. A mortal."

"Her *gifts*?" I stagger back a few feet, dizzied by the implications.

"You—the incessant whispers between you and Erron." Salt and tears lace my tongue. "The rainbow wine. You didn't touch it. You had a different flavor."

He inclines his head. "Yes."

I rake my fingers through my curls, almost tearing a few strands off my scalp.

His sheepish grin reveals his dimple. "I thought you'd be happy."

"And yet you didn't give me a choice." I whip back to face him. "You tricked me into drinking it."

The liquid he dared me to drink was thick and unusual. I didn't think twice about it because everything in Faerie tastes and feels different, but I remember how the aftertaste simmered at the back of my throat for hours, and how I thought Fae added strength potions to their cocktails.

"Erron agreed it was what Beth would have wanted. Her soul had to be freed either way, and the ritual had to involve a female mortal, so we figured it should be you," Cole says.

"What about what I wanted?" I croak.

He squints. "You wanted this. You've wanted it from the moment Flynn called you a dirty mortal. I saw it in your eyes—the thirst. You were never meant to live and die as a human. You came to Faerie with the horn. You married me. Why else would you say yes if you didn't believe it to be your bid at immortality?"

"It was *my* mortality—*my* choice—*my* damn life!" I cry out, grappling with the fact that my husband fed me a life-altering potion without my consent.

Immortality. I can't—

Shadows drape over his eyes. The sharp angles of his jaw quicken my pulse. "You told me you wanted to be queen. I didn't misunderstand that."

I throw my hands in the air. "We were mouthing off. Playing games."

"It was as close to telling you as I could get."

I grip my pendant and sink my nails into the skin, as though I can dig out the part of Beth he buried inside me. "I don't need you—or these *gifts*—I didn't ask for them."

"Gods, stop being so stubborn. We'll argue about this later." He shrugs as though I'm a spoiled child, and nausea turns my stomach.

I grip his arm to prevent him from moving. "Would you have married me if not for the infernal magic?" There it is. The question that haunts me.

Cole scoffs. "We're back to 'Cole is the villain of the story.' Really?"

I push on his chest. "You wouldn't have. I can see it in your eyes."

"Would you have married me if I wasn't a Fae prince?" He arches a cruel brow.

My mouth opens and closes. Fire heats my ears, and I want to slap the condescending pout from his face.

"You wouldn't have, and I'm not in a rage about it. I accept the truth. Whatever archaic notion possessed you to ask that pointless question —" He brings a hand to his heart. "I can't separate what drew me to you from what I feel now. I can't analyze if I would have fallen as hard for a Jules that doesn't exist. If you want me to lie and say, "yes, of course, sweetheart"—his voice sounds phoney as hell—"that's not who I am."

"You're above such things, eh?" My chin trembles. "And yet, you needed my magic to impress your father. What happened? Your pride couldn't bear the fact that you married a mortal?"

His lips curl in a snarl. "Hate me for now, if you must. I stand by my choice."

Somewhere between the lines, I lost sight of what the fight was really about, but I can't reel myself in. "Everything with you is a deal, an exchange of power. You say you love me, but if you really did, you wouldn't have kept this a secret. You would have given me a *choice*."

He grips my arms. "I'll give you a choice: either you step through that glass now and risk your life for people who don't deserve it, or you finally decide to hear me clearly. I need you. *Here*."

I twist in his grasp, freeing myself. "My sister is in danger. Lydia… My dad. You betrayed my trust, you should be grovelling for my forgiveness, not commanding me like I'm one of your subjects—"

A dry laugh grates his throat. "You are, though. You can't leave this realm without my assent." He's terribly beautiful in this moment, in this sacred room built by his people. The bunch of his muscles and the hollow curve of his lips quicken my breaths. Dark Fae power ripples along the walls, and the portals glitch to darkness, inactive.

Fear spikes in my blood. If he decides to keep me here...

"Your dad is useless and gullible. And your sister is a two-timing bitch. Wake up, Jules," he points to the empty mirror behind us, "you're running blindly into a nest of monsters."

Tears spill over my lids, my heart in pieces, the fragile trust between us shattered. "The only monster I'm afraid of is *you*."

Cole's nostrils flare, his cheeks hollow. His hands curl into fists, and his biceps strain. "Go ahead, then. See if I care." The lights of the hall of mirrors flicker on, but Cole barrels out of the room without looking back.

29

COME A LITTLE CLOSER

Jules

I gape at Cole's retreat. I crossed the line, but he had no right —I can't think. I press a hand to my heart, willing my pulse to die down to a manageable rhythm. Just when I can breathe again, an oily, lustrous shimmer appears on the wall at the back of the room.

I jolt into a fighting stance. "Show yourself."

Erron steps out from the shadows. "Remind me to return your wedding gift."

My teeth clench. "Leave me alone."

"I'm going with you, and there's nothing you can do to stop me." He spares me a wistful glance. "If you had asked for it, it wouldn't have worked."

Fists balled at my sides to hold in fresh fireballs, I ignore the old Fae.

"The unicorns added a failsafe to their ritual. To prevent sorcerers and dark Magus from hunting them to become immortal, they made it so the spell would only work on an unsuspecting recipient," he adds.

"That's an awfully convenient bail-out," I say, shaken. If it's true, why didn't Cole mention it?

"It sparked the legend of the unicorn and the maiden. A gift only bestowed on the ingenuous."

The inferno in my heart stills for a moment.

"How can I hope to live up to Beth? Cole should have known I didn't want to carry this burden. I didn't want this." I grip my emerald pendant and hold on to my anger for dear life.

Erron's mouth curves in a harrowing smile. "Didn't you?"

My heart pounds with the falsehood. I *craved* this, and yet...in the most twisted way, it robs me of my identity.

I'm no longer a mortal.

The Dark Falls' portal offers a wide view of the iron gates, and my chest squeezes. I square my shoulders and step through the glass.

Ice bites my cheeks as I emerge on the other side of the portal, but the tremors lashing through my body have nothing to do with the cold. Dark Falls' administrative offices tower behind the ornate iron gates. The moon lurks behind the clouds. Ravens fly across the sky, a delegation from the High Council forms a half circle in front of the entrance. Oz. Darkwood. Piper and—

My heart sinks past my feet, doubts entrenched deep in the rock bed of my very soul.

Oh no.

Dad.

My father scurries in my direction, and I straighten my plaid skirt. I wore my uniform, though I'm not sure why. I'm glad I didn't choose the Fae armor Cole suggested. That would have freaked Dad out big time. My mouth stings with thick, bitter saliva. When I first came to the Academy, I was a mortal witch, raised amongst humans. An outsider. I wanted to prove myself and justify Dad's efforts. Now, I'm an immortal, half-demon witch married to a Fae prince...

Two familiar arms wrap around my frame. "Munchkin, thank the Gods."

A shudder quakes my body, but I reign the panic in. "Dad." Tears crack my armor, but I swallow them back quickly. If I cry now, I'll never be able to stop.

Ambition and recklessness had molded me into something else entirely. I'm not ready to face him. How can he recognize me, when I'm not even sure who I am anymore?

"What did that devil prince do to you?" he asks, and the starkness in his eyes burns worse than the fire in my veins.

He's not talking about my newfound immortality. No one knows about that, yet. He's talking about the wedding. I guess Oz let that piece of news slip.

Dad narrows his eyes at my escort. "Erron."

"Councilman Winslow," the old Fae answers with a tinge of humour.

"You let this happen to my daughter?"

Erron scratches his stubble. "You haven't changed one bit, I see. Fae aren't the enemy."

"What do you want from her?" Dad places himself between us.

The Fae offers my dad a lazy shrug. "Young love rarely makes sense to old, fatigued warriors."

Dad snorts. "Love? Do you expect me to believe that's all this is?"

I wave a hand in my father's face. "Ask me, not him. I'm only eighteen, but I have a voice—and a brain."

Earth magic thuds through the air in loud, powerful ripples. "Where is he?" Dad searches the darkness behind us.

I square my shoulders. "I told him not to come."

"I want to speak with my daughter. Alone." Dad brushes off freshly conjured sand from his hands. Last time I saw him so angry, I was ten. I'd used magic to paint in front of the whole class.

Erron brushes past us to chat with the others.

Dad's voice quiets down. "I love you, Munchkin, but you don't know the first thing about Faerie or the Seelie court."

I grit my teeth. "I just came from court."

"You're under their spell. It's not your fault," he sighs.

I tug on my curls.

Despite my frustration with my father, I understand the paradox of Faerie better. To outsiders, the Fae seduce and steal mortals away to their realm. To the initiate, it's a fair deal, but as long as magic is involved, as long as Fae glamors exist, and their power stokes the flames of our hidden desires, how can anyone believe it's free will? Especially when our own society is built on the premise that lust is a sin.

And I'm a very pissed off sinner.

"Give me any antidote you want. I did this of my own free will. You need to listen to me."

Dad was dragged through hell for falling in love with my mother, and my birth reshaped his entire destiny. Surely, he can relate to what happened in Faerie.

"I'm listening."

I hug him and let tears mist in my eyes to present the picture of innocence. "Oz used angel dust on Cole to kill Miss Eillis. He's sleeping with Allie," I whisper quickly in Dad's ear.

The patient, patronizing gaze disappears at the sleeping with Allie part. I've got his attention now.

"Are you sure?" Dad scans the crowd.

The dragon chats quietly with his agents, their eyes fixated on us.

"Don't look at him." I wet my lips. "He used angel dust on me, too, but failed. That's why I left for Faerie. That's how I ended up marrying Cole. I'll explain everything in detail later."

The President closes in on us. "Come, Miss Winslow. It's time for you to honor our deal."

Dad squeezes my arm. "Do as he says, but I'll arrange for us to meet right after this. Don't worry, Munchkin. I'll get to the bottom of this."

I nod and follow Darkwood to the line of trees. The Magisterium agents follow us until we enter the forest. Oz doesn't follow, but the air of worry and doom written on his face doesn't soothe the ache in my stomach. What did Darkwood tell him about tonight? What's the official plan?

The vampire leans closer to my ear. "We'll close the tear first. After you give me the horn, I'll have Osbourne arrested."

I pause. "You'll expose Oz before I give you the horn. It's non negotiable."

Darkwood flashes his pointy teeth. "Fine."

I don't have the horn. I'll show trust by closing the portal first. Darkwood will unveil the truth about Beth's death. Once the dragon is arrested and his sins are exposed, it'll be too late.

30

THE FAE PRINCESS

$\mathcal{P}$erched on a tree above the tear between the realms where Jeremy's body was dumped, I wait.

And wait.

Jules' little blue dot reappeared on the Dark Falls' roster earlier tonight. I'd set alarm after alarm to ensure I'd be the first one to know, but when I arrived at the gates to meet her, hidden by the shadow of the trees, everyone had beaten me to it.

Darkwood. Mom. Dad. Daniel. Half the Magisterium's elite...

All the major players had reunited to greet my little sister. I couldn't fly closer to the huddle without being seen, so I decided to get VIP seats on the action instead. After they finish their little *chat* at the front gates, they'll end up here, where I can see and hear everything.

Once more, I've been stiffed. No matter how much I try, none of them cares enough to include me in their plans. When my thunder isn't needed, I don't exist.

Jules always ends up in the middle of the action, while I have to lie and cheat and hide in the fucking trees to be kept in the loop. Figures.

Arms wrapped around the trunk of a thick pine, I wait. The rough bark scratches my hands, and my muscles scream in agony before I finally see shadows move between the trees.

What the fuck?

A shine radiates off my sister as though her skin has absorbed the light of Faerie, but that's not supposed to last more than a few seconds on an earthling.

Their lips move, but I can't hear their voices over the high wind and curse under my breath. Careful not to disturb the branches too much, I slowly climb down the tall pine and crouch low, inching closer and closer to Jules.

A loud *whoosh* sends the dead leaves and branches flying. Jules stands with her palm open to the shiny black hole in the middle of the clearing. It's ten times smaller than it was a minute ago, and I hold my breath.

She can close an underworld portal.

My little sister.

Daniel mentioned that Beth had taught her how to do it, but seeing it with my own eyes... How is she summoning so much infernal magic? The stream of power emanating from her is ten times as strong as it had been in the Duel ring, and I can't comprehend where it's coming from.

The portal shrivels to a thin line, and Jules wipes sweat off her forehead. Laboured breaths quake her ribcage. "Give me a minute. I'll finish the job."

Darkwood shakes his head. "No need. I prefer it this way."

"Are you serious? Hollows might still squeeze through."

"As long as the Underworld portal is still active, it remains a threat. The people of this realm need a common enemy, not harmony. Empires aren't built on peace. Who do you think started the rumors of a Fae-Demon alliance?"

I shouldn't be surprised Darkwood wants to use the fears of his constituents to get more power, but if the hollows are as dangerous as Daniel implied, this is irresponsible—and crazy.

"Why are you telling me? Are you hoping I'll switch sides?" Jules asks Darkwood, her forehead creased in confusion.

The vampire cocks his head to the side, an eagle admiring a mouse, and my pulse spikes.

"Your husband didn't come today, why?"

Husband? Either Darkwood seriously bumped his inflated immortal head this morning or—No. Oh hell no!

"He didn't want to help you," she spits out with a little bit of sadness and a truckload of attitude.

Darkwood's lips quirk up in a hollow, vicious smile. "He's smart. You dangled the horn as the last piece of our agreement, but you don't have it, do you?"

I hold my breath.

Before I can digest the news of Jules' wedding—or move—Darkwood slides a shiny dagger from his jacket and sinks it deep into her side. The blade pierces her stomach without warning.

"No!" I blast off into a hazardous flight and ram my shoulder into the vampire. The strength of the push throws him off balance and sends him flying to his ass as I land next to Jules.

Lines creases her face, and she holds her hand to her side. Blood pours out of the gash in a thick, red ooze.

My breath catches in my throat, and I crouch to help her. "Wrap an arm around me. Hold pressure on it."

A large panther prowls out of the woods. With a growl, it bends down—front legs and head close to the ground—before springing above our heads in a jaw-dropping leap. The black flash of fur and teeth lands directly on Darkwood's chest, and I've glimpsed at the demon cat enough times to know I shouldn't look directly at it if I don't want fear to overwhelm my senses. I grit my teeth and concentrate on Jules.

Roars and curses thunder behind us.

The ancient vampire wrestles off the demon and launches it into a tree. A sickening mewl tears through the clearing.

He dusts off his pants. "Silly girl. Your mother told you to stay put."

"You promised not to harm her." Electricity buzzes up and down my body. Gods, if I have to fry my mother's boyfriend and the president of the realm, I'll do it. They promised me Jules would be safe. They *swore* no one else would die. What's the point of ruling the world if you have to burn it down to own it?

Darkwood dashes closer, his movements swift and assured. "Don't be a fool. Sacrifices need to be made. She's half-dead already."

Lightning sparks along my skin to warn him off. "Don't come any closer."

From the corner of my eyes, I see Jules' hand rise. Infernal magic buzzes through the air.

Darkwood bares his long canines. "I didn't want to do this. Your mother will be heartbroken."

I aim a bolt of thunder at his chest to hold him back.

The vampire's edges tremble with energy, and his magical armor absorbs my thunderous blasts. My blood runs wild. The small opening glistens in the moonlight, like a dark wound between worlds. My muscles cramp as I haul Jules closer to it and prepare a lightning strike.

Darkwood prowls forward, arms spread on each side, his razor-sharp nails scary as hell.

If he comes close enough, the energy from the tear might cause his armor to glitch, like I observed the other night. I watch the blue shimmer for my cue to attack.

His hand closes around my throat at the same exact time as his armor flickers, and I press my palm into the middle of his torso. The lightning whips him hard, and Darkwood staggers away, his back hunched like I just kicked him in the nuts. His frustrated holler scratches my ears, and the smell of crispy vampire flesh dries my mouth. Oh, I got him. I got him *good*.

"Little cunt. Look at what you did." He falls to his knees on the rock slab, one arm holding his front, but his armor is back in full force. He builds a yellow orb in his other hand—a death spell.

The demonic feline slithers to our side as though it wants to shield us from the deadly orb. My sister slumps to the ground, dark, burgundy blood pooled below her. I can't think.

I wrap my arms around her midriff. I can't get very far with her in tow, but this can't be the end. Before I form a real plan, I push all my magic forward, and fly us directly into what's left of the portal.

HOPE YOU ENJOYED Book 3 of Dark Falls. Jules' adventure in the Underworld comes next.

Pre-order Forgotten Monsters here: https://bit.ly/readForgottenMonsters

One witch to rule them all...

Lost in a realm full of monsters, I have only myself to blame.

Unfortunately, my trip to the Underworld will cost me more than I could have imagined.

Forgotten Monsters is the fourth and final book in Dark Falls Academy, a spicy paranormal fantasy series. Fall under the spell of Dark Falls gorgeous beasts.

Join my newsletter for exclusive, free stories: http://bit.ly/anyaslair

Want more right now?
Love sexy demons, sassy witches, and smoking-hot werewolves? Check out
Shadow Walker right after this.

LOVELY READERS

*T*o support me and the books, please leave a rating or a review on Amazon.

THANK YOU FOR READING. I wrote Forbidden Magic after I fell in love with Holly Black's Cardan. If you haven't read her amazing series, *The Folks of The Air*, check it out.

OMG, I'm going to find a cave to hide in with this cliffhanger. Don't despair, Dark Falls' fourth (and currently last) book will be out in May.

To keep up with my releases and receive exclusive extras, including bonus epilogues and special sneak peeks, join my newsletter.

Click here: http://bit.ly/anyaslair

Xoxo, Anya.

Connect with me on Facebook: https://www.facebook.com/AnyaJCosgrove/

SHADOW WALKER

ead the series that started it all! Fall for the shadows. Kiss the enemy.

Nothing stays black and white in a world full of shadows...

I'm Alana Mitchell, and for my twentieth birthday, I got a brand-new magical destiny instead of the laptop I was saving for.

I'm a witch. I have powers I can't control, enemies I know nothing about, and a legacy I can't begin to grasp.

There's a shadow-world out there waiting to swallow me whole, a world I didn't even know existed until I used my magic and unleashed hell upon my naïve self. From heart-eating ghouls to glamors, potions, and spells... nothing is as it seems.

A renegade demon and his brother are teaching me the ropes and driving me crazy with their I-know-better attitudes, beckoning stares and stupidly handsome faces.

At this rate, I'll flunk Witchcraft 101. I want to hunt down the bastards that destroyed my future, but the brothers' past is threatening to steal my soul and tear me apart—literally.

To survive, I must embrace the darkness simmering inside me and unleash the devil within, no matter the consequences...

PICK UP YOUR COPY NOW!
http://bit.ly/buyshadowwalker

MAGNETIC

Free on KU!

Who said life was a fairy tale? Because I'd gladly slice that jerk's head off.

I'm Vicky, though that's not really my name. Lying becomes second nature when you're on the run.

I never expected to end up half-naked in the woods. I didn't plan to stumble upon the most powerful shifter clan in North America and three of the sexiest men I've ever laid eyes on.

Dominic, the fun and reckless new wolf.

Sam, the hot doctor with glacial-blue eyes.

And Gabriel, the intense, secretive alpha who wants nothing to do with me.

My real name is a one-way ticket back to hell, and my secrets need to stay dead and buried like the girl I used to be.

Sleeping Beauty, Snow White, Red Riding Hood—I can be all three. I can use my powers to earn a place in their werewolf town, away from the bite of my past mistakes. I can use them—and their bodies—to survive.

The only thing I can't do is fall for them.

Magnetic is a stand-alone, steamy reverse harem romance featuring a kick-ass heroine and three swoon-worthy werewolves. Pick up your copy now!